Along the Wheel of Time

Sacred Stories
for Nature Lovers

REV. JUDITH LAXER

Along The Wheel of Time
by
Rev. Judith Laxer
Copyright © Rev. Judith Laxer 2016
Cover Copyright © Loretta Matson 2016
Illustrations by Patrick Corrigan
Published by Gaia's Essence
(An Imprint of Ravenswood Publishing)

GAIA'S ESSENCE

Ravenswood Publishing
Autryville, NC 28318
http://www.ravenswoodpublishing.com

Printed in the U.S.A.

ISBN-13: 978-0692736340
ISBN-10: 0692736344

Praise for
Along the Wheel of Time:
Sacred Stories for Nature Lovers

In Along the Wheel of Time: Sacred Stories for Nature Lovers the personal and the mythical intertwine, which is how sacred story should be. Page after page, Judith Laxer pours out the mystery of time and being like a wondrous broth and on it we dine. We are served nourishment through our seasons from her lips, from her heart, from the voices that move through her from beyond the veils of time.

-Normandi Ellis, author of *Awakening Osiris: the Egyptian Book of the Dead*

Judith Laxer's resonance with the deeply mysterious and often fantastic world shines through these lyrical stories, each held by an ancient celebration of seasonal renewal. Her imaginative tales are like a night around the fire with the wise and soulful storyteller goddess you've always wished for.

—Sonya Lea, author of *Wondering Who You Are*

CONTENTS

Dedication

Preface 1

Notes to the Reader 7

Yule 11

Imbolc 33

Ostara 57

Beltane 77

Litha 95

Lughnassad 115

Mabon 135

Samhain 165

Chants Used in the Text 183

Acknowledgements

For Pagan folk and nature lovers everywhere, who are doing their magick and cherishing Mother Earth.

4/19

Dear Katolen,

with deep gratitude
and much love,

Judith
xo

Preface

I HAVE ALWAYS WALKED with one foot between the worlds. As a child, I had such psychic experiences as knowing what people were going to say before they said it and what was going to happen before it did. I knew what the plants were silently saying. An elder family member who had

1

died came to me in dreams asking for my help among the land of the living. I thought this was just how it was, that everyone lived like this.

When I got a bit older and came to realize this is not how everyone lives, not what most people experience, I went into hiding—as much as a gregarious, outgoing, dramatic, spotlight-loving, performing artist can be in hiding.

Looking back now, I wonder if the drama I sought to create outside myself was a way to mask the drama within, a way to protect my sensitive soul in a world which gives credence only to what is seen with the eyes and heard with the ears. Because I lived in a way that was not shared by anyone I knew, it was safer to keep my spiritual experiences under wraps.

I was raised in a traditional, rather than a religious, Jewish family. This meant celebrating just the major holidays in family gatherings at which specific foods were eaten. It wasn't until I was an adult doing my own research that I learned the reasons for these celebrations. Although they made interesting stories, they never inspired the same spiritual awe in me as the sight and feel of the full moon or the world covered in snow or the brilliance of a sugar maple in October or the splendor of the first crocus in spring. The beauty and grandeur of the seasonal changes were more similar to my internal landscape than anything I encountered externally.

Nature elicited devotion in me. She gave me the knowing that the Earth was alive. That, like me, she had a soul. And we belonged to one another. This direct experience of divinity was quite different from what I learned about a distant and punitive God. I could not relate to that God. I could not understand or believe in original sin, and it certainly did not seem fair that it was the fault of women. So I quietly went on my way, keeping my spiritual sensibilities to myself, grateful to live in a family where religious practice was not expected.

I don't remember how I obtained my first deck of Tarot cards, but I know I had one by the time I was fifteen. I kept them wrapped in a silk scarf in a shoebox on the floor of my closet. I dabbled with them for years, and they helped resurface and strengthen my psychic abilities. In many ways, the wisdom of the Tarot introduced me to the mysteries of non-traditional religious practice, and helped me bridge the gap between psychic phenomena and spirituality.

But it wasn't until my late twenties, after much spiritual exploration, that I discovered Paganism. Here it was! The reverence for nature, the inclusion of the Divine Feminine, the magic! I not only felt I had found what my soul had been searching for, but that

I had returned to something precious, as if I were coming home. It made sense to me. I felt relieved.

Since then, I have consistently celebrated the eight sabbats on the Wheel of the Year and the phases of the moon in my spiritual practice. At the beginning, there were precious few reliable books on the subject. Through experimentation with others I met on the path, I learned how deep, beautiful, and life-affirming the practice of magick can be. I learned practical techniques for creating sacred space and raising and releasing energy, and came to love each season for its own beauty and significance in the cycle of life.

This spiritual practice changed everything for me, including what I do for a living. If you would have told that little girl— who woke up frightened out of her wits from a dream in which her dead Aunt came to ask a favor—that she would eventually earn her keep as a spiritual counselor, Tarot reader, and teacher of the mysteries, that she would become a Priestess of the Goddess and the founder of a thriving ministry for the Earth, she would have told you that you were dead wrong, that she was going to be a Broadway star and win the Tony award! She would not have believed you at all.

For years, students, congregants and friends have been asking me when I was going to write a book. However, by now so many books on magick-making are available. Does the world need another how-to book on the subject? I didn't think so. But then it occurred to me I knew of no books of fictional stories that depicted everyday people engaged with nature in a magickal way. No stories that could enhance sabbat rituals, or help readers connect to nature spiritually. So I began to write them.

These stories are intended to assist in deepening our connection to nature and the seasonal changes in our yearly journey around the Sun. Each one was written as an offering to those who live closely with and honor the Earth as the Divine Feminine, our Great Mother who gives, sustains, and takes life. The Great Mother who also provides the place of rest and reflection before birthing us again. Each story demonstrates, through the experiences of the characters, how the changing of the seasons is a spiritual model for the soul.

Circles have no beginning and no end, but seasons occur due to the earth's changing relationship to the Sun. For this reason, the first story in *Along the Wheel of Time* is for the sabbat of Yule. We begin here as the light emerges from the dark on the longest night of the solar year.

However, you may want to start with the story that is closest to the current season during which you will read it. You may want to wait for each sabbat to read the corresponding story, or read it as part of ritual celebrations. You may want to read the whole book through, and then return to each story in the proper season. My hope is that the stories bring your return year after year along the wheel of time. Blessed be.

Notes to the Reader

Listed below are the definitions and explanations of several terms used in these stories.

athame
A dull edged dagger used to represent the element air. Athames are often used to direct energy in the creating of sacred space when casting a circle.

besom
A broom used to sweep energy in sacred space.

between the worlds
Earth-based spirituality embraces the existence of non- ordinary reality. This term refers to the altered state of reality, sometimes called an energetic, that one may experience in magickal practice.

cone of power
By singing, dancing, chanting, drumming, etc., magickal energy is raised and directed toward a goal. This energetic is referred to as the cone of power.

deosil
Clockwise; the direction of increase. Used to build
energy in magickal workings.

magick
British Witch Dion Fortune defined magick as the
ability to shift consciousness at will. Within
Witchcraft, or the Craft of the Wise, the term
magick is used to describe the use of specific
energetic techniques to effect change in
ordinary reality. The 'k' that is placed at the end
of the word makes the distinction between this
spiritual practice and slight-of-hand or parlor
tricks.

pentagram
Five pointed star that is the symbol of Wicca. Each
point of the star represents the elements of this
nature religion; earth, air, fire, water and spirit or
ether. When this sacred geometric shape is
encircled, it is known as a pentacle.

sabbat

A sabbat is the spiritual celebration performed on the eight natural holy days that occur in one solar year; the solstices, equinoxes and cross quarter days in between. I have used the Celtic names for these sabbat stories and they are: Yule, Imbolc, Ostara, Beltane, Litha, Lughnassad, Mabon, and Samhain.

widdershins
Counterclockwise; the direction of decrease. Used to release energy in magickal workings.

Witch
The name for a female or male who has been initiated into the Craft of the Wise, and practices the art of magick- making as part of their spiritual life.

Yule

AT YULE, THE WINTER SOLSTICE, it is said that the great Cosmic Mother gives birth to the Sun, the light of the world. At midwinter, the days begin to grow longer. Pagans keep this sabbat holy by holding vigil through the longest night of the Wheel, keeping candles and fires lit to welcome the return of the light.

In this story, the magick of the sabbat ritual is interwoven with one woman's experience of giving birth to her first born. She has chosen a home birth, assisted by her husband, a midwife, and a doula. Desire to support, love and greet his child brings her husband to the birth. The midwife is there to facilitate the birthing process and catch the baby. The doula is there for the mother, providing for her needs as the birth progresses.

REV. JUDITH LAXER

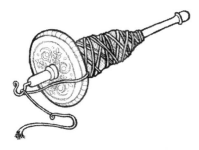

WHEN THE DEPTH OF WINTER was upon them and the Earth lay dormant, when the land was covered in snow and the cold crept indoors, held at bay by warm blankets, cups of hot tea and wood stoves, an earthquake began in the small   of Sophia's back.

She'd tossed and turned all the night before, feeling restless, unable to find a comfortable way to put her body. The blankets were too warm, her pregnant belly too heavy, and its pulling and tugging kept her awake for most of the night. And now, late morning, this spasm in her sacrum told her that her baby was on its way. As she had done a million times before, she imagined her birth canal to be smooth and wide, open and relaxed, but it didn't seem to ease the tension in her body.

She called to Brian.

"It's begun! Our child is coming!"

"Are you okay?" he asked, running in from the other room.

"I think so, she replied, "but it's intense! Should we   call the midwife, or wait?"

'What are you feeling?" he asked, as he had been instructed to do.

"My lower back is spasming and it goes down the sides of my belly."

"Is it constant?"

"No, but even when the spasm eases, my belly doesn't relax." "Let's wait until the next one and see if it's stronger, okay?"

He put his hands on her swollen, tight belly. "You're beautiful!" he said.

In the respite between quakes, Sophia found comfort in thinking through the journey of her pregnancy. She remembered how early last Spring she stepped outside in the melting snow and caught sight of the first, rich purple crocus with its jaunty orange center. She had smiled softly at the idea that the heat she and Brian had created together in their lovemaking the night before had provided enough warmth for a flowering. Six weeks later, as she wove the ribbon around the Maypole, she knew it for certain when she felt the quickening in her womb. Life had blossomed there and its presence elated her. Her belly grew with the Summer, and by early Autumn it was as round as the moon and just as luminous.

She marveled at the changes of her body: the dark brown, vertical line down her huge belly, how her faster-growing nails were stronger, how her skin seemed to glow. But mostly she marveled at her breasts! Always rather modest, they now swelled to a great size, heavy and sensitive, her nipples so very dark. "Getting ready to nurse," her mother told her. It was odd but wonderful to feel her baby kick from inside her. She imagined over and over what her baby was trying to tell her with those kicks, what her baby would look like, who her baby would be.

By mid-December, she felt that her body was no longer her own. She wanted to give herself over to being nothing more than a host for this life inside her, a resource of blood and fuel, food and lineage that existed only to grow and provide for this child. She had heard other mothers speak about how difficult the last few weeks of pregnancy were, how they wished to reclaim their bodies for themselves, how they longed to be over and done with carrying. But Sophia loved the feeling of her baby filling her inside, changing so drastically how she went about her days.

The next quake took hold. "It's hard to pinpoint," she told Brian. "I feel it everywhere. My belly cramps from the inside and tightens on the outside."

Her contractions went on like this for the better part of the day. Sophia kept walking around and around inside the house to keep herself busy, humming to calm herself and to show Brian she was doing just fine. By late afternoon each quake intensified and came a bit faster on the heels of the one before. They agreed that this was the signal to call for help.

* * *

Across town, Ruby Moon Circle meets inside the Temple sanctuary, arriving before the rest of their community. They greet one another with warm embraces, anticipating another experience of soulful magick. Tonight is the celebration of the Yule sabbat, and preparing the central altar is a ritual in itself.

Everyone takes hold of an edge of a large red, round cloth, helps lay it on the floor in the middle of the room, and places cuttings around it: fragrant cedar for protection and evergreen holly for the return of life. The cardinal directions hold the four elements: a crystal for earth, an athame for air, a candle for fire, and a chalice for water. In the center, a freshly crafted, evergreen wreath represents spirit, the hub of the Wheel, where all things connect. A basket of candles waits in the southern quarter of the circle.

As they complete these preparations, others start arriving wearing warm and soft clothing for the long night's vigil till dawn. They carry food and drink to share and sustain them through the night. Before long the flurry of greetings gives way to a focus on the reason for the gathering, and everyone gathers around the altar in the center. The ritual begins.

***

Jill the midwife and Maggie the doula arrived within minutes of each other, half an hour after twilight. Jill was a clear, tall, warm woman of middle years, with short salt and pepper hair, experience in her eyes, certainty in her presence, and a comforting tone in her voice. Maggie wore soothing greens and browns, her silver-threaded plaits hanging down her chest. Sophia thought Maggie was psychic, knowing everything there was to know about exactly what you were feeling and when. When they had interviewed Jill, it had been clear she respected Sophia and Brian's spiritual path. Maggie already followed a magickal path. The two women were the perfect people to assist in the birth of this child.

Jill checked Sophia's progress. Her capable hands prodded a bit, but were not invasive. Sophia found her touch reassuring. After the initial examination, Jill said, "Great. It's all going perfectly. Nothing more to do but wait."

Jill and Maggie watched Brian pace, as he asked questions they had already answered for him. They shared a glance. Jill spoke up.

"Brian? This would be a good time for you to start boiling water and warming the towels. And if you would brew a pot of strong coffee and prepare any other food you think we'll need as we wait, that would be great."

She smiled as Brian's face registered relief at her request. He fairly leaped to accomplish these tasks.

Brian was a wonderful man, a devoted husband, and eager to become a father. But Sophia knew that idleness felt unnatural to him, especially under stress. She smiled back at Jill, grateful she'd given him things to do.

The burning wheel of the pale sun had long since set as the bed was prepared for the birth. The bedroom was fast-becoming sacred space. Maggie lit a smudge stick of sage and quickly blew the rising smoke in the four directions, north, east, south and west, before snuffing it out. Then she lit a candle scented with frankincense and myrrh and placed it in the center of the bedroom altar. They all settled in for the long winter's night.

Humming softly, Maggie propped more pillows behind Sophia. With gentle hands she removed the barrette holding Sophia's hair and drew the brush against her scalp, sweeping it into a neat shine without a single knot or tangle. "This will make the birth easier." she said, her eyes twinkling magick. Sophia sighed contentedly and Maggie could feel her relax.

***

Now, the High Priestess offers her hand to the person standing to her left and one by one they clasp hands around the circle, encompassing the altar.

"Let's take a deep breath together. As you exhale imagine a line of energy reaching from the base of your spine down toward Mother Earth. Feel as She opens to receive your taproot, and send it down further until you feel deeply grounded in Her."

She pauses, sensing as everyone in the circle follows her instructions.

"Now, draw strength from our Mother, pulling Her up through your grounding cord and into your heart." She pauses again. "And now, draw power down from the Moon and Sun, the Goddess and

God, and feel the silvery and golden light as They enter into your crown and make Their way into your heart as well."

The High Priest continues. "Let's take another deep breath together and on the exhale, direct this energy from your heart into your hands, and send it deosil around our circle."

He waits until he feels the energy return to him. "Our circle is cast in perfect love and perfect trust. Blessed be!"

A Priestess holds up the crystal as all turn to face the north. "Spirits of the North" she says. "Power of Earth, laboring Mother of us all, we invite you into our circle! On this, the longest night, we stand with you as you bring the Sun to glorious birth. Be here now. Blessed be!"

***

Jill came back into Sophia and Brian's room as the next spasm took hold, and peered intently between Sophia's legs to determine the progress. "Good." she pronounced. She checked her watch and made a note.

Now a Priest in the circle holds up the athame as all face east. "Spirits of the East", he says. "Power of Air, joy and relief of breaking dawn, we invite you into our circle! On this, the longest night, we breathe with you as you bring the Sun to glorious birth. Be here now. Blessed be!"

Out of her big tote bag woven of hemp she'd spun herself and dyed with beet juice to a deep brownish red, Maggie took her athame and placed it under the bed. "To cut the pain in advance," she said.

***

In the circle at the Temple, another Priest holds up the candle as all face south. "Spirits of the South," he says. "Powers of Fire, shining star in the heavens, we invite you into our circle on this the longest night.

We radiate with you as you make your way through the Mother to your birth. Be here now. Blessed be!"

Sweat trickled down the side of Sophia's face and beaded above her upper lip.

"It's too hot!" she exclaimed.

"Turn off the heat!" Jill instructed Brian.

"You're kidding!" he said, standing in the doorway of their bedroom. "I'm freezing!"

"Put on a sweater." Jill answered with calm authority.

***

A second Priestess holds up the chalice as all face west. "Spirits of the West" she says. "Powers of Water, lifeblood of the sacred womb, we invite you into our circle on this the longest night. We open our hearts with love to keep you in the flow. Be here now. Blessed be!"

***

Sophia's belly rippled once more as her breath caught and a rush of warm liquid soaked her loins. For a second, she wondered if she had lost control of her bladder.

"Your water just broke!" Jill said, blotting the amniotic fluid with a towel. "You're doing great."

Sophia's heart pounded in her chest. She knew there was no going back, and she hoped it meant they were getting close.

***

The High Priestess and Priest step onto the altar and clasp hands in the center of the circle.

"As the Goddess is to the God!" she says.

"As the God is to the Goddess!" he replies.

Together they intone, "So the two conjoined bring blessedness to life. Mother Nature, Father Time, we invite you into our ritual on this the longest night. Be here now. Blessed be!"

***

Maggie pulled a chair up beside Sophia's bed. She reached into her tote bag once more, and this time took out her spindle and a large clump of raw wool. After she attached a piece of the wool to the spindle, her arm rose, and the spindle dropped and began to spin. She loved this tool. The spinning would help Sophia's brain waves to focus. Maggie started humming an easy tune.

Sophia watched transfixed as the spindle spun around and around, as something new formed from the mass of fiber, a thin, smooth strand of wool that wrapped around the spindle in neat and evenly spaced rows.

Maggie added on another piece as her arm rose again, and the spindle dropped again in a slow and steady rhythm, creating a relaxed atmosphere of predictability.

Sophia's breathing slowed and steadied, her pulse calmed.

***

"Tonight we gather to hold vigil as the Goddess gives birth to Her Son, the Sun, the Light of the World." The High Priestess's voice is clear and strong. "Our energy raised in song will help carry Him through the birth canal. Our candle lighting will symbolize the return of the light. We know the Sun will return at dawn whether we keep this sabbat or not, but keep it we do and in this way we support the Great Mother as She labors. We stay focused on the miracle of birth and the miracle of our Earth in her orbit. We experience the mystery of   new life beginning as well as the mystery of the life sustaining cosmos. Blessed be."

"Blessed be!" comes the resounding echo.

***

Another contraction and a loud gasp.

"Are you okay?" Brian asked, wide eyes in his anxious face.

Jill placed her hand on his shoulder. "Brian, why don't you pull over that chair and stay closer to Sophia? She's doing great. No need to ask that question again."

Then he remembered. He wasn't supposed to ask a stupid question like "Are you okay?" If anything, he could ask specifics: "Can I hold your hand? May I put another pillow behind you? Do you want a sip?" "Are you okay" was really a question he was asking to reassure himself.

Brian wasn't sure he wanted to pull up a chair and stay closer. That was the plan they had agreed on, but now that capable Jill and magickal Maggie seemed to have it all under control, he wondered if he might lose his cool as the labor progressed. He worried that he might be in the way instead of helpful, or that he might faint at the sight of the blood he knew was surely coming. But he drew up the chair anyway, sat down, and put his hand on Sophia's shoulder. He wanted her to know that he would not abandon her. "I'm here." was all he said.

The contraction eased. Sophia breathed a deep sigh. Jill nodded.

***

In the circle, the basket of candles is passed and each person takes one. The High Priestess starts to sing the call and response chant.

Celebrate the return of the Sun.
Light the way, oh Sun King!
Dance the round on Solstice night.
Blessed be the Great Mother!

She walks toward the candle in the south and lights hers from it, then shares the flame with the nearest person. The flame passes from candle to candle around the circle. Light grows. Eyes glow. Voices strengthen the chant. Energy starts to flow and builds from person to person. The feeling of love envelops them all like a warm wrap on this cold night.

***

Maggie began to spin again, catching Sophia's attention once more, as Jill checked and announced that Sophia's cervix had dilated to seven centimeters.

"Is that good?" Sophia asked Maggie in a hoarse whisper. "It's perfect!" Maggie said, smiling.

***

One by one, the lit candles are placed in the center of the wreath.

Light the way, Oh Sun King!

***

Another contraction, more intense.

Maggie said, "I am adding a new color!" causing Sophia to look at the spindle again. Maggie knew the spinning would keep the all-encompassing at bay just a bit longer.

***

Now all the candles blaze together in the center of the circle. Some folks sit by the fire meditating on the return of the light. Some continue to sing as they begin the traditional spiral dance. Soon the serpentine dance winds around and provides the chance for each to make sweet eye contact as they pass one another.

After a while, some dancers drop out to rest and meditate, while those who had been sitting join in the dance. The calm of rest alternating with the energy of the dance keeps the magick flowing. Everyone has a place in holding vigil on the longest night.

***

Brian dozed in his chair. Maggie walked Sophia around and around the room, and then sat her back down to massage the pressure points on Sophia's legs that would trigger the release of the infant from her womb. Jill sipped her cup of coffee and the night wore on.

The journey from seven centimeters dilated to the birth of her child took patience, endurance, courage, and the rest of the night. Sophia knew that at some point, she would have to surrender herself to the great waves of pain and movement that she could not control. As if on cue, her body grew active once more, this time with a vengeance. She gripped the bed sheets as her breath caught.

Brian awoke and shook the sleep from his head. "I'm here, Beautiful!" he said.

The contractions were coming faster now. Sophia could feel her muscles push her baby lower and lower and she knew she was on the brink of the visceral and magickal miracle of birth. She was acutely conscious of her blood and sweat and breath, all of it real and unashamed and unwaveringly present. Time was suspended, exhaustion carried sway, and she was amazed by the natural wisdom of her own body.

Tears streamed from Brian's eyes. He felt awed by witnessing the greatest feat a woman can perform—the giving of life. He gently blotted the sweat from Sophia's forehead.

Jill said, "On the next contraction, push!"

"Oh, my Goddess!" Sophia cried out, her staggered breath coming through gritted teeth as the contraction took her.

Maggie, her arm around Sophia's back, encouraged her, "Lean into the pain and use it!"

"Use the pain?" Sophia thought wildly. "How do I do that?"

And as if she had asked the question out loud, Maggie answered. "Push into it. Don't brace yourself against it. Push into it!"

And then everything clicked. Sophia's body understood what her mind could not imagine. The next wave roiled from within. She took a deep breath and bore down into the blinding pain.

Jill announced, "You're crowning!"

***

More candles are lit now until every one of them is aflame, increasing the light and the heat, and the chant is sung to the ring of fire.

Blessed be the Great Mother!

***

Sophia was panting now.

Jill said, "You're doing great, Mama, the next one should do it!"

And then the next contraction began. It was too much. Sophia struggled against it. She had to stop the pain, to disengage from it.

Jill said, "Push!"

Sophia cried, "I can't!" but her body took over. The baby's head pushed toward the light—but then receded.

29

"Help me! My baby!" Sophia sobbed. "Help me!"

Maggie took Sophia's face in her hands and turned it toward her own. Their eyes caught and Maggie said, "I know you can birth your baby, Sophia. I know you can! On the next contraction, push your baby outside of your body."

"Here we go!" Jill almost shouted.

Brian and Maggie flanked Sophia on either side of the bed and supported her as the final intense wave crested.

"Now!" Jill cried and then the sound of pure human will filled the room.

Sophia gathered every ounce of her strength and her voice sang a high steady note as she pushed the head of her precious baby out past the gateway of her sacred body.

In the circle, voices collected, singing together, a joyous song of celebration and relief, rising to meet the dawn.

ALONG THE WHEEL OF TIME

Imbolc

AS FEBRUARY BEGINS, the sabbat of Imbolc heralds the Spring. Although temperatures are typically still quite cold and snow often lingers on the landscape, the Earth begins to stir and awaken and quicken the growing season. Early flowering cherry trees and hardy crocus are a welcome sight after a long Winter of limited color.

At the resurgence of Mother Earth's energy, Winter begins to fade. Pagans celebrate by blessing seeds for the upcoming season of growth, and by dedicating themselves spiritually. Sometimes this comes in the form of committing to a spiritual community, to a spiritual practice, or to a specific Goddess or God. This resurgence also brings a time of initiation, the rite of passage that is a symbolic death of the old self and a rebirth of the new. The deep significance of initiation has a profound effect on the spiritual seeker when it is chosen consciously, after a period of time engaged in spiritual exploration and practice. An important part of an initiatory experience is an ordeal, when a fear is faced and conquered or a hardship is endured to test one's faith.

In the following story, we witness a Witches' coven during a magickal woman's initiation by a test of faith brought about by a healing crisis. The initiation is facilitated by her loved ones and spiritual sisters and culminates as Spring brings hope and renewal.

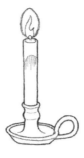

FIVE YEARS INTO Vera and Kelly's love affair, Kelly was diagnosed with multiple sclerosis.

She first sensed it as pins and needles that crawled up from her ankles to her calves, and no amount of massage, chiropractic, or even acupuncture relieved the feeling. At first, she thought she had just injured her ankles dancing. She still danced a great deal, even though her career had shifted in the last few years from performing in musicals to teaching dance classes, and choreographing musicals. She rested her legs whenever she could, stayed off and soaked her feet, had her students demonstrate the dance steps instead of doing them herself, and took frequent naps because she often felt tired.

After two moons, the symptoms persisted and she began to worry and wonder if there might be something more serious going on. When she woke up with blurry eyesight one morning, Vera made an appointment for her with one of her own colleagues at the hospital. She and Kelly went to it together. A few weeks later, the news was so disturbing that Vera came home with the results to tell Kelly herself. The diagnosis was MS.

"I don't get it. How did this happen to me? I always take good care of myself! If there is no definitive test for MS, how can they be sure what it is? And how are we ever going to know how to handle this or what to do?"

They lay together in the afternoon sun that streamed in through their bedroom window, Kelly's head on Vera's shoulder, tears falling from her eyes.

It was late Summer, just after Lughnassad and the early Autumn light was turning syrupy and golden.

"We'll figure it out." Vera replied, in the carefully composed and soothing doctor's voice she used with patients all the time, although her stomach was in knots and she was filled with dread. "We'll follow the protocol for MS and if that doesn't help, we'll know it's something else and we'll keep trying until we get it."

Kelly sighed and snuggled deeper into Vera's long body, comforted by the confidence in her voice, grateful to have such a devoted partner. They might not have stood at the altar to speak their vows, but surely here was the "in sickness and in health" part, and her faithful lover, the strong, beautiful, dark haired woman beside her was the best spouse any woman could ever want.

"Let's call the Witches, too." Vera added. "Our circle can create a healing ritual for you. How does that sound?"

It sounded good and soothed Vera as well just to suggest it. Their circle of spirit sisters called themselves the Daughters of Selene Coven, after the lunar Goddess. In the three years since they formed their coven, they had accomplished powerful physical and emotional healing for one another in their magick-making together. They had seen each other through easy and difficult times, and their frequent journeys between the worlds had strengthened their bond as well as their magickal skills.

"We'll ask them at our meeting next week." Vera spoke this as if saying it meant the cure was already on the way. It made them both feel better.

Not for the first time, Kelly marveled at the complexity and polarities of her lover. Vera had been raised in a devout Catholic family, and had talked to Kelly about how she'd felt both protected and constricted by the stringent tenets that held her. As Vera had matured she'd realized that she didn't have to leave her history completely behind in order to create the life she wanted. Now, for all her alternative lifestyle, Vera was as conservative politically as any right-wing capitalist you could ever hope to meet. She worked as an allopathic doctor at a major hospital in town. Yet she was a member of a Coven and practiced magick. Here was a woman who was clearly in the sexual minority, and yet she held tight to many quite traditional values.

They had talked about the possibility of having kids early on in their relationship, but the idea quickly cooled when they discussed the kind of parents they'd want to be, how they'd want to raise them. Vera believed in very strict boundaries and in what Kelly thought was too-harsh discipline. In Vera's opinion, a child shouldn't learn about the birds and the bees until way older than Kelly thought was appropriate. To Vera television was the devil incarnate. Kelly had reminded her that they had turned out okay for all the TV they had watched as children, but Vera's voice had hardened as she responded that television was more innocent when they were young. Vera had a lot of rules about how a child should be raised that Kelly didn't agree with. It was clear to both of them that their parenting plans were just too different. After a while, all conversation of starting a family ceased.

But their differences worked well in all other aspects of their relationship. Vera provided stability, security, and structure to their lives, not to mention she was a patient listener, a fantastic ballroom dancer and a great cook. Kelly provided color and music and fancy, not to mention that her green thumb kept the house full of lush plants and their plates and cupboards full of treats from her prolific garden. Vera calmed Kelly and Kelly motivated Vera, and each loved the other with a fierceness neither had ever felt before for anyone.

Six years ago, they had been introduced at a Yule celebration by mutual friends who had rightly thought they would be perfect for one another. Both still pretty new to the Wiccan path, they had found themselves standing shoulder to shoulder in the circle. Kelly was enchanted with the sound of Vera's voice as she sang, and Vera won unknown points with her for holding the melody when Kelly shifted to the harmony.

Vera became enamored with Kelly's bright eyes and easy laughter and she felt like Kelly was a breath of fresh air in her otherwise predictable life. After the beautiful candlelit ritual, they had spent the entire time at the potluck feast talking and flirting. They'd exchanged telephone numbers before their reluctant leave taking that night and by New Year's Eve, they were deeply in love.

Their coven met at Beth's home the next week. Five women comprised their circle and when everyone arrived, they created simple sacred space. The coffee table became an altar holding the elements of magick: a stone in the north, a feather in the east, a candle in the south, a chalice in the west and a wreath in the center. They settled in with cups of tea as Beth's cats, Isis and Osiris, took their usual spots on laps. As at every meeting, they checked in with one another by passing the talking stick.

When it came to Kelly, she began to sob as she choked out what the doctor had said.

"I can't believe I have to tell you this, but I have MS! That's what all the pins and needles are about." She felt so vulnerable that it was hard to get the words out. "I hate to ask, but I wonder, I mean, maybe we can, you know, do a healing ritual for me?"

Upon hearing this news the women joined hands, faces grave and concerned. The two closest to Kelly held her shoulders so her hands remained free to gesture as she talked and cried. The touch strengthened their circle, and brought comfort and relief and a grateful sense of being in it together.

They spent the rest of the meeting planning a healing ritual. Rachel looked at her calendar and suggested that they have it on the weekend just before Mabon, because the dark of the moon flipped to new on that Saturday evening. This meant they could use the lunar phases in their magick, releasing the illness on the dark, and starting the recovery on the new. It was agreed.

Meanwhile, Kelly had already begun a few practical things that Vera and her Doctor had suggested to help her condition: changing her diet to cold-water fish and fresh fruits and vegetables, increasing her complex vitamin B, and adding in as many oats as she could to fortify her nervous system. Every morning breakfast was oatmeal and she drank no less than a quart of oat straw tea a day. She began to meditate in earnest, and rest went from something she guiltily stole to something that became a planned for priority.

In a few weeks, the blurry eyesight cleared, and although the pins and needles didn't disappear, they eased and were no longer constant. Everything shifted in her life. The things that were important to her became an absolute priority and things that weren't important fell away. It was a simpler life, less complicated and busy, more thoughtful and conscious. Her biggest challenge was going from obsessing about having MS to denying that she was ill. She and Vera talked a lot about that.

Kelly, swimming between hope and fear that the healing ritual would and would not work, was also afraid Vera would tire of the subject; that she would grow weary of the burden and turn away. Vera was afraid that Kelly would stop her new and diligent healthy routine and would worsen sooner than she needed to. MS became the thread that wove through the action of their lives. They could even pick up a conversation in the evening that had begun in the morning, when the clock told Vera it was time to go to work and Kelly to meditate. MS was something they shared even though it occupied only one of their bodies.

The coveners arrived at Vera and Kelly's home in late afternoon on the dark of the moon after Lughnassad. They brought specific items for this ritual, including a bag of organic compost, spring bulbs and shovels and trowels. After greeting one another, they set to work.

Kelly referred to one of her flower beds as the Moon Garden because she had planted it with nothing but white perennial flowers and silver leafed plants. It was the perfect bed for what came next. The women helped lift out and transplant some of the perennials elsewhere in the landscape until a clearing had been made. Then they began to sing as Kelly dug a pentacle shape in the soil.

Oh, Great Mother, Hear us calling.
We, Your daughters, seek healing.
Power, power, Your love is our power.

It took a while. A pentacle is not an easy shape to create: all five lines equally placed, and a full foot deep. They took turns digging until they were satisfied with it.

Back inside, they cleaned up and talked over the ritual, making sure they had all the items they would need. Kelly arranged the elemental representations for the ritual: her favorite crystal for the north; for the east, a pretty painted fan Vera had given her in their early days with a note that read *I'm your biggest fan!;* her silver chalice for the west; a wreath of willow for the center; and a candle she had previously prepared for this ritual for the south. While meditating on releasing whatever had caused her condition to occur, she had carved the candle with the symbols for hexing, disruption and banishment, and then had anointed it with some of the healing oil their coven had made a while back at one of their craftier meetings. Nearby, there was a bowl of thirteen raw eggs and an empty cooking pot, a large pitcher of water and a small bowl of sea salt.

Then the formal magick-making began. They created their sacred space by casting a circle and invoking the elements in each direction.

Beth said, "This evening we gather to heal our sister with our magick and love." She held up the bowl of large brown eggs. "These eggs will serve as the magnets that will draw her illness out of her body and then contain it, leaving Kelly disease-free. Blessed be!"

"Blessed be!" they all responded.

Kelly removed her robe and lay naked on a pile of soft blankets spread smoothly on the floor in the warmth of the wood stove; the rest of the women sat around her. Rachel led everyone in a guided visualization in which they walked down a long flight of stairs into a sacred room. There they wrapped themselves in layers of light that shielded and protected them while strengthening their power to heal.

When the visualization was complete, the women began to sing the chant again.

They kept singing as each of them took a raw egg in hand. Slowly and gently, they rolled the eggs on Kelly's body. They focused on her spine, legs, and feet, but made sure to roll them everywhere else as well, including her head and face.

Oh, Great Mother, hear us calling.

We, Your daughters, seek healing…

The chant became a round, and as each of the eggs became full from the energy of the illness, they became noticeably heavier. One by one, when the eggs could hold no more, they were placed in the empty pot, until all of them were used and their singing ceased. Vera softly spoke Kelly's name.

Kelly lifted her head. "Is it done?"

"It's done!"

Kelly stood, her body moving as if pushing through thick honey. The women wrapped her fluffy white terry cloth robe around her. Andrea handed her the pot and Kelly held it, looking down at the eggs that had taken the illness from her. They seemed to pulse. Or maybe it was just her own heartbeat as it thrummed loudly inside her.

Now it was time to use the elements to further the magick. Beth asked the element air to blow the winds of change through this situation and they blew their collective breath onto the eggs. Andrea asked the element of earth for purification as they tossed sea salt onto them. Rachel poured the water over them as she asked it to wash Kelly clear of pain and suffering, and then Vera took the pot from Kelly's hands and put it on top of the wood stove to cook, asking the fire to transform the illness into health.

As they waited for the eggs to become hard boiled, the women shared some bread and apples to fortify themselves.

"How do you feel?" Andrea asked Kelly.

"Good. Weird. Clean."

She was still a bit in the trance of the magick. Vera put a protective arm around her.

When the eggs were cooked, they turned the water on in the kitchen sink and poured the water from the egg pot into the stream from the faucet, watching the waters join and run down the drain, steam rising, until only the eggs were left. Kelly got dressed in warm clothes and, taking up the pot of eggs, she led everyone outside to the moon garden in the manner of a funeral procession. The women stood around the garden bed and watched as Kelly planted the eggs, widdershins and deeply, into the pentacle they had dug earlier.

"I release any hold this illness has on me, any hold it has on my body. I release my fear and the upset this has caused. I release any attachment I have to it. I leave it behind me now. MS no longer has me in its grip. Blessed be!"

When she was done, Vera handed her the shovel and she covered them with compost, giving the illness to the earth to compost, too.

Wiping the dirt from her hands, Kelly turned away from the garden to walk inside once more. The women trailed her and following magickal protocol, no one looked back. Andrea spied the clock on the way in.

"Quick!, she said. "The moon is about to turn!" Vera grabbed her besom to sweep the last of the illness's energy out of the circle as Beth lit some sage and waved the rising smoke into the air.

Round and around and around about,
sweeping all the illness out!

They passed the besom widdershins, chanting until they felt a shift in the energy of the space and the moon slipped into her next phase. She was new.

They settled down on the floor once more, with Kelly sitting in the center holding the basket of spring bulbs. Rachel led them through another visualization down a different flight of stairs to a room with pots full of liquid colors of the rainbow. Beth started to drum a simple rhythm and the circle began to hum. Soon harmonies floated in and they chanted pairs of words such as mighty strong, my sister, morning star, and magnificent sight to replace the doom-like "multiple sclerosis".

Before long the shift in the energetic was palpable. Everyone in the circle could feel the magick, each so perfectly in sync with what they were doing that no one had to consciously think about their actions. They had found the right groove and the work became effortless. In this liminal place, holding the intention for the outcome was all that was needed for the energy to carry it to its goal. The women wove the magick together, amplifying it. Flicking their hands toward her, they tossed the colors of healing they had gathered between the worlds onto Kelly as they danced around and around her, singing out her new reality. Kelly let herself becoming a living sponge, soaking up the healthy images given to her by her spirit sisters.

The energy shifted again. The tempo of the drum sped up and voices intensified in response to the raising of the cone of power. The women knew when it peaked and together, using their will, they directed the cone down onto Kelly and the basket she held. Hearts beat rapidly in chests, breath came heaving, arms reached out, palms directed toward the center as the last of the energy seeped through them and into Kelly. Kelly allowed herself to fully receive it.

As the feeling of energy faded, the women ate more apple slices to help bring them all back to ordinary reality. Usually they shared a feast after releasing the sacred space, but tonight Kelly wanted to sleep immediately following the healing. She lovingly placed the bulbs on their bedroom altar before she crawled into bed. And there they stayed for the next full lunation.

Vera and Kelly followed an old practice of holding silence about the magick until it manifested. They trusted that the ritual magick was now working between the worlds and would come back in its time, bringing with it their intention, or what they often called "this or something better".

The new moon fell close to Mabon and the coven gathered again. It was a Monday evening and the air was crisp with impending Winter. Twilight filled the air as the women created the sacred space for the next part of their healing magick.

Kelly led the processional out to the garden again, this time holding the magickally charged bulbs in their basket. The women began to sing the healing chant.

> *Oh, Great Mother, hear us calling.*
> *We, Your daughters, seek healing.*
> *Power, power, Your love is our power.*
> *Power, power, our love is our power.*

As the chant continued, Kelly placed the bulbs deosil atop the more deeply buried eggs. One by one, she planted them, knowing that the transformed illness would act as fertilizer for the beauty of the mighty strong woman and the magnificent sight these flowers, and she, would become. When the rest of the compost was added on top of each bulb the planting was complete and the magick was done.

It was a very different Winter. Slower. Quieter. Restful. Vera and Kelly chose to decline invitations to most of the Winter holiday festivities and discovered a different kind of beauty in reading to one another, exploring the flavors of different teas, and watching the Winter birds outside their dining room window through binoculars. Samhain passed, and then Yule. They spent New Year's Eve at home, over a bowl of hot soup, the crackle of the fireplace logs providing emphasis to their loving conversation. The Wheel of the Year turned.

Two weeks before Imbolc, the coven met to plan their sabbat. It was the time for honoring the Irish Goddess Bridget and Her gift of holy flame and healing waters. This first sabbat of Spring, the time of the quickening of the earth, when the sap began to rise in the trees, and the bulbs began to stir beneath the ground, was when devotees of the Goddess made or renewed their dedication to their spiritual path. A time of Initiation; a symbolic death of the old as rebirth occurs for the new.

Kelly had been mentally preparing for her dedication at this sabbat since Yule, and its importance eclipsed any other she had ever made.

As Vera drove them to Rachel's home for the sabbat ritual, Kelly leaned her head against the cool glass of the car window, watching the world go by. She realized something. Ever since she had been diagnosed with MS, her observational skills had increased. Maybe it was the possibility of the disease robbing her completely of sight, or eventually of her very life, that had heightened her desire to track the details of her life that she might someday miss.

Now she noticed everything. That morning she spotted buds on the hydrangea in their front yard, saw that the primrose flowers had appeared, bright pink in sharp contrast to the long gray of Winter. Driving along she counted seven oaks growing like sentinels along the way, last year's reddish brown and crinkly leaves still clinging to the branch, secure until the growth of new leaves would push them off. Getting out of the car at Rachel's, she noticed the daffodil shoots emerging from the soil, moss growing between the stepping stones, and the skeletons of last year's bright geraniums standing bravely and bare in the container pot before the porch. She noticed the broken spider web up in its corner by the front door, the dead spider somehow still clinging to it. She noticed the smooth feel of the button as she rang the doorbell.

They were the last to arrive and were welcomed with strong hugs. Coats were hung and soon they all gathered around the altar, which was set with white lace over a dark green cloth. In the center stood a black cast iron cauldron. Over the standing lamp shade was the Bride's veil, a round circle of white tulle trimmed with shiny silver satin that would be used in the ritual.

Deep and lengthy quiet during the Winter had helped Kelly plumb her own depths. In the long stillness, she had journeyed into her heart and soul and body, and had discovered what the eggs, now deep in the earth, had taken from her, what they had been holding: fear and anger, and then guilt over getting sick.

She found what was gestating in the healthy flower bulbs; love, forgiveness, and finally blessed acceptance. She discovered that acceptance gave her more power over her health and happiness than fight or struggle did. She came to embrace the actions needed for her health as an expression of self-love, rather than a medical protocol needed because something was wrong. And now in the Imbolc circle, the profundity of her dedication quickened Kelly's heartbeat. Having her spirit sisters witness her dedication to the Goddess would help integrate her internal with her external reality.

The circle had begun and the gestures of welcoming the early Spring were shared: the washing of one another's hands with the Goddess Bridget's healing waters, the lighting of the purifying flame within the cauldron, the blessing of candles representing the growing light. Finally, it was time for the women to make their dedications.

Rachel went first. Kelly placed the veil on her head and over her face. Rachel chose to make her dedication silently; the women stood in the peacefulness as Rachel spoke to the Goddess in her heart. When she was finished, she took the veil and placed it over Andrea, who spoke her dedication with conviction. Beth went next and then Vera, each woman placing the veil on the next. Kelly watched her lover's face beneath the veil and the firelight reflected in her dark eyes.

"This is what Vera would look like as a traditional bride," she thought. "Gorgeous!"

She felt so much love for Vera that she thought her heart would break because it could not hold it all.

Vera dedicated herself to better using her intuition. She was tired of the pendulum of her life swinging so severely from mundane to magickal and back again, and was ready to implement this gift at all times, not just when she was in the safety her home or their magick circle. She would start doing so even on the job. Especially on the job.

When she finished her dedication, she turned toward Kelly's loving gaze and stole a quick kiss as she drew her lover under the veil with her before stepping back and out of it.

Kelly adjusted the veil and looked into the holy flame. She took a deep breath feeling the strong presence of the women who stood in the circle with her, the women who had cast the healing spell with her and had supported her healing journey ever since.

"Great Goddess, Mother of us all, Blessed Bridget," Kelly began. "I dedicate myself to You tonight as a healer. I know that I must heal myself. I know that I am healing myself, and I know that healing does not always include a cure."

She paused, the meaning of the words hanging in the air. "I trust You, my Goddess. I trust You even when I relapse fearfully, even when I dread what my mind conjures up in my imaginary future, I trust You. I trust that You have not given me this illness randomly. I trust that what You have given me has a divine purpose. I accept that this condition is a permanent part of my life even as I accept that it can be completely healed. I dedicate myself to healing, to being a healer, to Your healing ways, so that by healing myself, I will heal the world. Blessed be my dedication, for the highest good of all. Blessed be."

The next morning, Kelly walked outside to her moon garden. She delighted in noticing the green shoots emerging from the pentacle in the soil.

ALONG THE WHEEL OF TIME

Ostara

AT OSTARA, the renewed life force ascends to the surface of the Earth. The Vernal Equinox brings equal day and equal night as we enter the light half of the year. Nature resurrects and vibrant color returns to the landscape. The days are growing longer and warmer, and now it is time to clear the cobwebs of Winter's stillness, sweep away lethargy and taste the freshness of Spring on each breath.

This story is of a daughter's springtime awakening, not merely to the season, but to a new life she chooses for herself from the wintery depths of loss, sorrow and withdrawal.

May 11

Dear Mom,

Martin fired me today. Economic downturn, budget cuts, blah, blah, blah. He and I both know I am barely present at work. I keep missing meetings and taking sick days and everyone else on the team is picking up the slack for me. I am grateful Martin has kept me on this long. I actually felt worse for him than myself today in that sad, stressful meeting. He gave me a whole month's notice but I immediately packed up my desk and left. It was a great relief to hear the door close behind me.

The days are coming and going but I am barely tracking them. Today I looked at the calendar and it registered that Beltane came and went without my realizing it. I don't think I could have joyfully danced the maypole anyway. I seem to have no energy for any of my usual Pagan rituals. Mother's

Day also came and went but I am glad I didn't track it. I am already a mess.

I finally went to the post office and picked up a huge bag of your mail. Most of it is junk. The mailman told me to draw a diagonal line across your name and address, and then write "deceased" next to it and put it back in the mail. This way when it is returned, your name will be taken off the list. I asked if there was a form I could just fill out to stop all mail to you but he told me that your name would continue to be sold to other junk mail lists, plus then I wouldn't get other mail that is important. But I find it too hard to write the word "deceased" over and over beside your name, so I started writing "no longer living at this address". Perhaps your address should now read "Summerland, realm of the afterlife."

Love, Elaina

June 18

Dear Mom,

It's Father's Day and I find myself wondering why I never asked you the millions of questions I still have about Dad. I keep wondering if it would have been better for me had he died after I was old enough to form my own memories or if it's better that I never knew him. I wonder how you managed to carry on after he died. I guess having me to take care of removed the option of falling apart. Thank God I don't have any kids! I can't imagine having to be there for anyone else, feeling as I do.

The lawyer called to "check in" with me. She wants to know if I've given any thought to selling your house. I told her no. I have given thought to nothing.

I promised my best friend I'd go to the movies with her today. She wanted to stay away from her brother- and sister- in-law and their badly behaved kids who "dysfunction perfectly," as she puts it.

She actually had the nerve to say to me, "You don't know how lucky you are to be an only child!"

"Bess," I said, "I'd do anything for a sibling right now!"

Then she started to cry, and told me that she'd be my sister and the whole thing disintegrated from there. So I told her I changed my mind and just wanted to stay home. This made her feel even guiltier and cry even harder. So now I am stuck going when all I want to do is sleep.

Everyone is so happy about the Summer, but I hate the heat. Everyone is so happy about the sunshine, but it hurts my eyes.

I guess you and Dad are together again, huh?

Love,
Elaina

July 5

Dear Mom,

I thought someone was shooting off a gun last night! Then I heard a loud whistle before an explosion and I realized it was fireworks. The whole neighborhood was going at it. Didn't help my headache. I had to close the windows to shut out the noise, but then it was too hot to sleep.

Aunt Claudia left me a message. She went over to your house, but forgot her key. She was hoping I was home and would come over to let her in. I was home, but I didn't pick up. I think it was a ruse to get me out of my place and over to yours. But I can't.

Love, Elaina

August 20

Dear Mom,

I had a craving for the pancakes at our diner. I wasn't sure I could go there alone but I did it anyway. Sue and the others all cooed over me when I walked in and it made me feel very self-conscious. Then I read the menu like I'd never seen it before and Sue waited to come over until I put it down. I ordered pancakes like it was a novelty, like she didn't know I was going to. I didn't have the heart to ask for "the usual" as we always did. When she patted me on the shoulder before walking off, it was all I could do not to lose it sobbing. But I managed to make it through the meal and get out of there without falling completely apart. I left feeling as exhausted as if I'd run a marathon. I don't think I will go back.

Bess is having her end-of-summer barbecue next Saturday, and she wants me to bring my homemade potato salad. I haven't cooked anything since you...left. I still don't know why you left. I couldn't cook anything right now if my life depended on it. Bess has a new man she wants me to meet, and to entice me she said he makes a mean strawberry Margarita. I know I am not going, but I haven't told her because I don't want the fight.

I took a walk the other day and caught sight of someone reflected in the picture window of a store whose mismatched clothes didn't fit, whose dirty hair hung in her eyes, and thought, "Holy cow, lady! Who dressed you this morning?" Then I realized I was looking at myself. I guess I need a haircut, too.

Love, Elaina

September 21

Dear Mom,

Last night I had the most amazingly vivid and detailed dream I have ever had, and you were in it! In the dream, I walk for several days to get to a familiar place that I don't actually know. I am welcomed by several women who take me into a bathhouse. They take my dirty clothes, and I walk down a few steps into a beautifully tiled bathing pool. The fresh water is warm and it soothes my tired body. There are bowls of fruit, bread, and clean water to drink.

The scene shifts and I am dressed in a simple linen robe, walking in a long line of people, up a hillside, scarlet with poppies, and around an impressive building that I somehow know is a

63

holy place. There are seats carved into the hillside and soon we are all sitting, theater-style, looking down at a stage. There is a performance going on. I don't remember the details of it, but it is very dramatic, and, along with the rest of the audience, I gasp and shout and laugh and cry and wail in response to what is being shown to us.

I notice that while the performance is taking place, people are being led backstage, one at a time. When it's my turn, a man escorts me out of the theatre and into a huge temple space. It is magnificent. Full of clean lines, and lit only by candle and torch. At the entrance, he dips his finger in a small bowl of oil and marks my forehead with it. He leads me into the center and leaves me there alone. I am not sure what I am supposed to do, so I stand there, taking the place in. The altar holds a silver cup, a basket with a half shucked ear of corn, and an open pomegranate, its blood-like juice having pooled on the marble.

A Priestess approaches and guides me through a door into the inner sanctum.

"When you are ready," she tells me, "knock on the portal to the Holy of Holies."

When I do, the door opens by itself. An older Priestess sits waiting for me. I don't remember what happened next, except that I was embraced so tenderly and she told me things I swore to remember but now cannot. I leave feeling special, renewed, and blessed, like I have been given a great gift.

I expected to leave this sanctuary and go back into the temple but instead the same door opens to the outside. It is daylight, in a busy village square and you are sitting on the wooden bench that surrounds a central well. It has been so long since I've seen you, Mom! It was as real as if you were actually there! I step in closer to look at your face, into your eyes. You look so sad. The sorrow in your eyes caused my tears to flow. You look directly at me and say "Come home! Come home, Elaina!" And then I woke up.

So good to see you last night.

Love, Elaina

October 27

Dear Mom,

I don't know why I can't pull it together. When Kathy's dad died, she was back at work and more productive than ever two weeks later. But I can barely seem to get out of bed in the morning, and I've been going to bed earlier and earlier at night.

Emulating nature is part of my magickal path, and I know we are on the brink of entering the darkest eighth of the year, but not being able to stay awake is over the top! Your accident was way back in the Spring (I still can't say "you died"), so I should be better by now. I should be getting used to being so alone.

Samhain is a few days away and I can't even think about making an Ancestor altar. I don't think I could bear seeing your photo on it. I think this is the first Samhain in my entire life that I am not enchanted with the season, the pumpkins, the black and orange of it all. Some Witch I turned out to be.

Back in April, after the memorial service in your living room, I washed the dishes, threw out the rest of the food, and locked the door. I haven't gone back. The lawyer helped me set up automatic mortgage and utility payments from your estate. She even set up automatic rent payments for my apartment. I never did a thing with your garden. I imagine all the vegetable starts you put in are rotting nicely by now, or going to seed, food for the birds and squirrels.

I hope the kids stay away from your house on Samhain. Maybe they will think it's haunted.

Love, Elaina

November 29

Dear Mom,

Aunt Claudia kept inviting me for Thanksgiving and I kept declining. She wouldn't take no for an answer and ended up coming over to my apartment with a roasted turkey that afternoon. I was taking a nap. I could see how upset she was to find me still in my robe, the house a mess, the garbage stinking up the kitchen, but I wasn't expecting company. It was awkward and uncomfortable and I couldn't wait for her to leave. I felt bad for her. She is used to your clean house, good cooking and pretty china. It didn't even occur to me that my only aunt, single herself, would want to spend the day with me, now that you are gone. Truthfully, I had forgotten all about the holiday until she called, asking about my plans. We ate the store-bought food together. She asked me if I had any plans for your house and I mumbled something about selling. She said she'd be happy to help with that, and then finally she left.

Once the words were out of my mouth, I thought it was a good idea. Why not sell? Maybe then I could buy my own place, stop paying rent, start a garden of my own. Maybe even move away and start over. There's nothing here anymore.

Love, Elaina

December 31

Dear Mom,

I'll not be sorry to say goodbye to this sad year, even though it was the year you were still here with me, when I could call you any time and talk, drop by any time and be welcome, or meet you at our diner for pancakes. Oh, Mom. I miss you so much I can't stand it.

Today I caught a whiff of something foul and wondered, "What's that smell?" And it was me! I took a very long, hot shower and then did three loads of laundry. At the grocery store everyone was saying "Happy New Year! Happy New Year!" and I just wanted to scream at them all to shut up. I'm making oatmeal for dinner, then going to bed. Can't wait for the holidays to be over and done!

There is a little bit of snow still on the ground outside. From my window, I can see the tire treads in the road and the winter birds up on the telephone wire in the cold. It's warm and cozy inside. I think I'll light a candle.

Love, Elaina

January 1

Dear Mom,

Woke up early this morning into a new year. Spent the day reading the paper, making split pea soup, ignoring the phone and the message Bess left me. I feel like I should be doing something, but I don't know what. Guess I could start looking for work, but I really can't even think about having to go to a job and interacting with people every day. I am really grateful that you left me so well taken care of. I don't know what I'd do without your money. Probably get evicted and end up on the street.

I keep thinking of selling your house and all that I'd have to do to get it ready for sale. If I feel up to it, I'll go over tomorrow and take a look. I don't want to go alone, but I don't know anyone I'd want to go there with except you. And that is not an option, is it?

I probably should find a real estate agent and get some advice. There's a snow storm predicted so that might mean I have to wait. Feels weird just writing about it. What am I supposed to do with all your stuff? Selling it seems so mercenary, giving it away so heartless, even if I gave it to a good cause. I can't keep it all, but I don't know how to handle it. I'm sure Aunt Claudia will want some things, and I do, too, especially the hutch, the green antique vase, and your china. But what about all the rest? Just the thought of your garden tools makes me cry, knowing you'll never use them again.

Love, Elaina

February 7

Dear Mom,

On Imbolc last week, I promised the Goddess Bridget that I would start to address your estate, so today I called Aunt Claudia's real estate agent and put your house up for sale. Then I called a company that comes and takes everything left from an estate, and booked them to come to your house in two weeks. Maybe I should have booked it for a month from now, but I thought this deadline would help to motivate me. Why do they call it a deadline? Why don't they call it a living line?

Yesterday, I finally went over to your house. I felt like I was walking back in time. Part of me expected you to answer the door. The stillness of the place was unnerving and it seemed colder inside than out. I could actually see my breath. I turned on the heat and then wandered from room to room for a while until it was warm enough to take off my coat.

There was a layer of dust on everything and all your house plants are dead. Sorry. I had forgotten all about them. Forgotten that anything alive remained. I made myself a cup of tea and sat down at the kitchen table to sip it while I listened to the silence in the house. Then I grabbed a dust cloth from under the sink and began to dust the furniture in the dining room, then the living room, then the guest room. Before I knew it, I had gone through the whole place and dusted everything. Then I thought I should finish the job, so I vacuumed the house. Next, I called and ordered a small pizza to be delivered, and cleaned the bathrooms while I waited for it to arrive. I think your house is clean enough to show to buyers. Not sure I can get it cleared out before anyone comes to look at it, but that will have to do.

I sat in your chair and looked out the big kitchen window into your yard and garden. At the few birds. At the wind moving the empty branches. At the snow-sopped leaves on the garden beds. It will probably be good to have the house sold and to move on. Too many memories here.

Love, Elaina

March 19

Dear Mom,

So much has changed in the last month. It's hard to explain why, but this is how it occurred.

A few weeks ago, after cleaning your house, I went out to your garden for the first time. I walked around looking at all the beds and stopped in front of your asparagus patch. I remember you telling me that asparagus are one of the earliest spring vegetables. I felt compelled, so I grabbed handfuls of the soggy leaves away and the stubs of a few new asparagus shoots were hiding underneath! My heart started to race with excitement at the sight of the soft, fresh, green beneath the leaves. The smell of the sweet, damp earth brought tears to my eyes, and I realized that for the first time since you died, one year and three days ago today, I was crying with joy! I ran inside your garden shed and got your small hand rake and knelt down on the wet and cold ground to clear the bed of the last vestiges of Winter.

I stood staring down at the bed, with its dark brown soil, and the fat earthworms I had disturbed on the surface,   and then at the baby asparagus shoots. The more I looked, the more there were. It was as if they were popping up from underground as I watched, like stars appearing as twilight surrenders to the night sky. It was an intoxicating sight. And for the first time, I began to understand the depth of your joy in the garden.

I looked around again and everything seemed different. Now I wasn't seeing just garden beds, but the intricate design you had created. I could see that the rocks for the borders of the raised beds had been very carefully selected and placed. I noticed that your small orchard of fruit trees was planted strategically, that the trellises with the awakening wisteria and honeysuckle softened the lines of the fence, and that the compost pile had sunk a few feet into itself.

I turned to look back at your house, wondering what time it was and if I should be getting home. And then I had another thought.

I am home.

So I walked around to the front and lifted the "For Sale" sign out of the ground. I called the real estate agent and told her to take it off the market.

And then I called the lawyer to draw up the papers to transfer the deed into my name. Sold.

Tomorrow is Ostara. And here is my sabbat ritual plan. I am going to clear that small section of grass beside the garden shed and start my own garden bed. I am going to dig a very deep hole in that bed. I am going to take your ashes off the mantle inside. Then I am going to plant you in that bed, in the garden you loved so much, and the garden I promise to tend with all my love. Then I am going to sow thousands of tiny poppy seeds there. Now, while the temperature is still cool.

And later when they bloom, I'll make a bouquet of the delicate flowers and bring them inside to put in a vase. And when the pods dry, I'll keep the seeds to sow next year and the next and the next. Welcome home.

Love, Elaina

ℬeltane

BELTANE, THE TIME TO CELEBRATE the Union of Goddess and God as They become lovers, is the beginning of Summer and lies halfway between the Spring Equinox and the Summer Solstice, when the lush beauty of the Earth blossoms in all Her glory. The traditional Maypole dance is a metaphor of this union. Atop the pole, which represents the phallus of the God, each dancer ties a ribbon. Then a wreath of fresh flowers, representing the yoni of the Goddess, is placed there. The pole is erected and the dancing begins, every other dancer going deosil or widdershins around it, weaving their magick as the wreath slowly descends. This is the dance of the *Hieros Gamos*, the Great Rite, the Sacred Marriage.

During Beltane, the veil between the worlds opens, just as it does during Samhain, its opposite on the Wheel. At Beltane, the portal opens to the realm of Faery, the magickal place where time runs differently, where anything and everything is possible, where otherworldly light shimmers, where longings and desires are satisfied.

This story follows a young woman into her Mystery School as she learns about sexuality within this spiritual context.

REV. JUDITH LAXER

DIANA HAD BEEN TRACKING the moon more closely ever since she became a woman six months ago. Having recently turned twelve, she was among the youngest in her class who had come of age. She felt proud to mark a small red dot on the wall calendar in her room each month when she welcomed her wise blood. Today she counted fourteen days since her last blood time, and knew this meant she was probably ovulating. Diana marveled that the time when her fertility was heightened was the same time that sexuality was going to be taught in Mystery School. It must be the magick of the Goddess!

Mystery School was so very different from regular school. Here the teachings were inspired by the mystery and beauty of the Goddess, and the lessons were held within a spiritual context, not among the facts and figures of mathematics and history. The girls had been learning all about the Blood Mysteries; fertility, sex, pregnancy, birth, and menopause, not only as the basis for more deeply understanding the Goddess as Maiden, Mother and Crone, but also as a way to nurture and support who they were becoming as mature and responsible women.

Violet and Stacia had taught this level of Mystery School for several years and they made a great team. Small-boned Violet, with fair skin and clear grey eyes, always wore something purple. "To support my name and show off my red hair!" she joked. Stacia, with olive skin and a broad smile, towered over them all, her chestnut braids swinging as she walked. The girls loved them.

In Mystery School, they were taught reverence for their bodies and respect for the miraculous way their bodies could create and grow another life. They learned that the onset of their monthly blood meant they were fertile. They learned how to experience their monthly blood time as holy, how to retreat from daily life to honor it. They learned ways to increase their chances of pregnancy if they so desired in the future. They learned how to prevent unwanted pregnancy and the mysteries of abortion.

They had been taught about the act of sex. Actually, Diana had learned about it when she was a very young child from her older sister, who had come home one day and blurted out to her that the man puts his penis inside the woman's vagina and nine moons later, a baby comes out. Diana remembered being confused because she thought the penis was used to pee. Worried about this new information, she asked her mother if men's pee could make her have a baby. The next hour was spent clearing up a few misunderstandings.

Their mother told them that the penis also releases seed for new life on special occasions, that only those who love one another should have sex, and how important love is for the experience to be a good one. But she didn't talk about why love would make it a good experience, and she said nothing about sexual feelings in the body.

About a month or so after Diana's first blood, she woke up from a dream in which she had been galloping on a horse, her body flooded with bliss, her heart pounding quickly, her yoni wet. She didn't know quite what to make of this wonderful feeling. Secretly, she hoped the dream would return. When her blood arrived for the first time and the ceremony welcoming her into womanhood was held, the talk was about fertility, the possibility of becoming a mother one day, and the importance of self-respect and good self-care.

No one had talked about what sex felt like. This aspect of womanhood remained a mystery. She was excited because she knew today's class was not just about sex, it was about sexuality, and she hoped to finally get some answers.

Diana walked the three blocks to the Mystery School. It was in the center of her community, behind the Temple for the Goddess and had one entrance for girls and women, one for boys and men and one central door for everyone when larger gatherings for both sexes were held.

Today, Diana entered through the women's door. She found her cubby hole in the wall, kicked off her shoes and placed them on the shelf. Through the next door, she found the altar. The painting of the Goddess, pregnant with life, beamed down at her from the wall above it. As she had been taught, she lit a candle there to symbolize that her spirit was present as well as her body. Diana loved doing this. It was more than just being trusted to work with fire. She felt like the Priestess that she hoped to become one day, standing there at the altar, knowing what to do and what it meant.

Hearing voices and laughter coming from the next room, Diana was eager to join in. Classes were held only twice a month, and sometimes it seemed like years between gatherings with her teachers and friends in this sacred way.

When all the girls had arrived, Violet and Stacia called their class to order by starting the song:

We all come from the Goddess
And to Her we shall return
Like a drop of rain,
Flowing to the ocean.

Every class they had taken in Mystery School since they were toddlers had begun with this song, which always put them in the right mindset for embracing spirit. Before long, everyone was focused and the creation of sacred space began. The central altar was consecrated. A circle was cast. The directions and elements were invoked. A poem one of the girls had written to the Goddess was read, and the talking stick was passed so that everyone had a moment to relay what was on her mind or going on in her life. When they had been little, getting used to the talking stick was difficult, and the girls had trouble with interrupting. But now it was second nature to show respect by quietly listening, as well as by not talking for too long when it was your turn.

Diana was the last one to speak. She told the others that all she really wanted to talk about was her horse dream, because she had not been able to stop thinking about it and wondered why it had happened and what it meant—and how to have it again.

81

Violet thanked Diana for sharing something that made the perfect segue for today's topic, the mysteries of sexuality, and continued, "Of course, you have to experience a mystery to truly know what it is."

"But," Stacia said, "we can certainly explain a few things so you know what's going on when it's happening to you! Some of you have shared with us about your strong and loving feelings for some of the other boys and girls that you know. I am sure every one of you has had a crush on someone somewhere along the way."

Diana thought of Steven in her writing class. Heat rose in her body and she blushed scarlet. She remembered how their hands had touched when he dropped his pencil and they both reached to retrieve it, how he jerked his head to flip his sand-colored hair out of his eyes, how he had smiled at her with that lazy-looking smile he often wore.

Violet spoke next. "The feelings that begin in the heart can, and do, travel in the body. The onset of your wise blood each month lets you know that your body is preparing for these strong feelings. They can make you want to experience a physical closeness with another person."

Stacia picked up the thread. "In Dion Fortune's 'Charge of the Star Goddess', she speaks as the Goddess, telling us that all acts of love and pleasure are Her rituals. She created our bodies such that we can feel great pleasure by touching and being touched. We all know how good it feels to get a hug from someone we love. When we mature, those feelings intensify. Nature insures that life will continue by making sex so very pleasurable. When we are having sex, the friction and intensity our touching bodies create together can make us feel like we are going to happily explode! This blissful feeling is called an orgasm. It is a great and beautiful mystery that shows us how all the aspects of ourselves—the physical, mental, emotional and spiritual—can meld into one experience."

"Your dream," Violet said, looking at Diana, "was your body's way of showing you what an orgasm feels like. We can each bring ourselves to orgasm with our own touch. You should experiment and learn what your body likes in preparation for making love with someone else in the future. And when that future arrives and you fall in love with someone who also falls in love with you, and you decide to make love together, it can be the most beautiful experience you might ever know. Because making love is a sacred mystery, it is best to treat it as such. Just because it is happening through your   physical body doesn't mean it is not also a holy experience."

"Beltane is almost here," Stacia said. "We know this as the time when the Goddess and God make love and the fertile Earth begins to flower. This sabbat, marking the seasonal shift from Spring to Summer, can also be seen as a metaphor for the shift in maturity from innocent child to experienced adult, as in the following story."

Stacia walked to the altar in the center and rang a chime.

When the bell-like tone stilled in the air, Violet began.

In the late Spring of her early womanhood, a ripening Maiden felt the pull of creation. If someone were to ask her what she means by the pull of creation, she would say that she feels it in her body, in her hips, in her yoni. She would say that it feels like a tug and also like a spark. She would say that it spurs her on without knowing where she is to go. She would tell them that she knows it in her heart, that it shines in her eyes, that it moistens her lips. She would say that it smells like flowers, that it tastes like honey, and it looks like the sunlit morning after an endless night of rain: fresh, alive and growing.

For as long as she can remember, the Maiden has wanted to explore the forest at the edge of the meadow, to enter its green depths and experience the magick of the flora and the fauna. Until recently, she had always been too young to do this alone, and for some reason, it seemed that the true magick of the forest always hid itself, becoming invisible whenever she cajoled an elder to take her there.

She imagined the day when she would be free to go there by herself, to follow the trails looking for trillium in the shade of the forest's canopy, to whistle to the birds as they flitted to and fro, to taste the sweet, juicy berries that grew in the wild. She dreamed of the safe and hidden depths of the forest that would eventually welcome her and her first lover.

But life goes on as it always does, with work to do, lessons to learn, and repairs to be made. And much as she wants to drop everything and let the lure of the forest win, the Maiden heaves another deep sigh and tries to quiet this pull of creation, to concentrate on the tasks at hand.

At the very moment that the Maiden sighs, Pan awakens with itchy horns. He rubs them against the rough bark of a tree, which feels very good, but offers only temporary relief. Earth has moved again and Pan feels stronger than ever. Soon the itch spreads beyond his horns until it stands squarely and certainly between his powerful and cloven-hoofed legs. If someone were to ask Pan to describe this itch, he would say that it both itched and tickled, that *it was insistent, that it wouldn't let him think clearly. He would say that it felt like liquid flame, that it quickened his breath and it kept him from standing still.*

For what seemed like forever, Pan had waited for the Maiden to grow up. It was becoming difficult to remain patient. From his hidden vantage point in the depth of the forest, he dreamed of the future. Season after season, Pan witnessed as she grew and matured into a young woman. These last few seasons had been almost unbearable as the Maiden finally reached her coming of age, when her body and mind changed so completely and she began to long for a lover.

Now Pan catches an intoxicating scent on the breeze, and recognizes it as hers. To soothe himself, he reaches for his wooden pipe, nestled where two branches form a nook. His large and thick-nailed fingers wrap around it with reverence, as if it were a rare flower.

Holding it, he feels a bit more in control. This is something he knows he can do. He cannot change how he is feeling— the season rules. Desire-driven, he paces the forest floor, hooves meeting earth in a dance of anticipation. He scratches the base of his horns again and tries to bring his focus from the stiffness at his loins to the instrument in his hands.

He ventures as close to the edge of the forest as he dares without being seen, blending in behind a tree. Through the window of the house beyond the forest, he catches a glimpse of the Maiden with her cherry-colored mouth and silky hair. At the sight of her, Pan sighs into the pipe and a clear low note permeates the silence.

The Maiden suddenly feels compelled to step outside and takes a deep breath of fresh Spring air.

Pan matches her breath and blows a hauntingly sweet, simple tune through his pipe. The music conjures a faery, who hovers there, taking Pan in, knowing what he wants.

Soon the forest is alive with animals, birds, and a beautiful, green snake that glides around and up the trunk of a huge, old tree. The music from Pan's pipe has all of them enthralled. The faery swoops back and forth, drinking in and capturing Pan's magick spell, and then flits off to cast it.

Thrice the faery flies above and circles the Maiden's head and then darts back toward the trees.

Enchanted, the Maiden follows. As she looks before her, she spies an intriguing movement in the thicket. Before she enters, she stops and kicks off her shoes. The Earth feels warm and soft beneath her feet, and when she looks down, the faery is holding one of her shoes in its long and delicate fingers.

Their eyes meet and when the Maiden blinks, the faery spreads her colorful, shimmering wings and flies back into the grove, showing the way, shoe in hand! The Maiden steps into the grove to follow, and is immediately surrounded by Pan's sweet music. She stops at the sight of him.

There he is, playing his pipe: big, taller than she is, with limpid eyes, a pointy nose and beautiful curly hair. She gazes on him, astonished to see that he has the upper body of a man but the lower body of a goat! She feels the pull of creation again, sharp this time, tugging at her inside and she bites her lip to counter its intensity. She has heard stories about Pan, but never really believed he existed.

Pan takes the pipe from his mouth, and looking directly at her, he asks, "Believe it now?" His merry laugh is contagious and it prompts hers. The air is filled with his scent—green pine and aged leaves—and it makes her head spin.

She feels heat rising up along her spine and warmth spreading between her hips. Her heart beats faster.

Holding her gaze, Pan slowly brings the pipe to his lips once more and plays a pierce–your-heart melody. And when it is over, he walks to the Maiden, who, enraptured by the song, stands spellbound. He bends down, his face close to hers for the kiss.

Electric! The spark shoots through them both as their soft lips meet, their mouths hungry. When the kiss ends, he offers, and without hesitation, she climbs up on his back. He begins a gentle run, taking her deeper into the grove.

Her ears are filled with the sound of his hooves on the forest floor, the rhythm hypnotic. She rides his wildness and he carries her beauty as he runs, deeper and deeper into the green lushness, the pull of creation urging them forward. He speeds on, powerful and sure-footed; she clings to him with all her might. The forest becomes a blur, the world their own.

He slows to a stop, she slides off his back, they sink to the earth, face to face, heart to heart, the puzzle of their bodies a perfect fit. The magick eclipses their thoughts of anything but one another as Summer enters the year.

Love makes a Goddess of the Maiden. Soon, she hears the music once more as Her lover blows his sweet breath into the pipe. She feels light and happy and rises to her feet to dance. She feels different in her body, as if she has a secret. She loves his eyes watching her as she sways to the tune. She takes a ribbon from her hair and weaves it around the nearest tree.

When the story ended, the room was silent for a moment. Then Diana let out a delighted laugh, and the girls looked around at one another with shining eyes and mischievous smiles. Violet and Stacia exchanged glances, too. They knew this was only the beginning of their teachings on sexuality, but it was a good start and enough for now.

Litha

THE TWO SABBATS OF SUMMER, Beltane and Litha, center on the Divine Couple and the maturation of the season. At Beltane, the Goddess and God as Maiden and Horned One make love for the first time, and innocence gives way to knowing. During the next six weeks, this maturity grows and the solar year peaks. At Litha, the Sun King reaches His zenith of power, and along with glorious radiance comes the responsibility of all kings—that of giving his all for the good of his people.

On this sabbat, the flirtations and perhaps awkward first couplings of Beltane mature, and the Goddess and God make love with more than just their bodies. Their hearts, souls, and spirits merge, and their ecstatic union brings blessedness to life.

In this story, the zenith of the Sun's power is reflected in one woman's journey beyond her comfort zone to the realm of spiritual responsibility and transcendent bliss.

THE DRUM ROLL had begun. In the meadow, the meditating women were collectively jolted out of their calm and jumped to their feet. Noon was fast approaching, the sun was almost at its apex, and the sabbat ritual was about to start.

Since sunrise, these women, in pairs and triads, had walked round and round, flattening the grass and wild flowers with their bare feet, belled anklets ringing, creating a circle of magick, singing together.

> *He is golden, golden is He.*
> *Pour Your light, pour Your light*
> *Down onto me.*

Before long, the birds sang harmony with this chant, and if you were there, listening with your soul, you could hear the trees at the edge of the meadow singing, too.

Molly's heart beat faster in anticipation. As a child she'd stood with the elders at the edge of the circle. When she came of age, she joined the other teenagers in the group of musicians. Fifteen years ago when she reached adulthood, she became one of the early rising women who came to prepare the meadow for the ritual.

But today something felt different from all the other sabbats, and Molly knew why. She held the ritual secret and it filled her like a balloon, making her lightheaded and ready to fly.

Two days ago, her final preparations for the ritual had been interrupted by Kevin's ardor. He had come home particularly frisky that night. She smiled to herself as she remembered how he had come up behind her as she stirred together the last batch of cornbread, grabbed a handful of cornstarch from the bag and slowly rubbed it up her arms, across her collarbones and down inside the front of her blouse. The silky feel of the flour and the rough skin of Kevin's palms cupping her breasts, made her gasp. She loved that his desire for her was still so strong that it suddenly eclipsed the task at hand. She loved how their love had not settled into the less erotic comfort her friends talked about with their mates. She loved how they still made frequent, enthusiastic, adventurous love that continually revealed themselves to one other, keeping them connected in a way that was about more than just keeping house, community service, and sharing finances. Their love was still romantic, still flirtatious, still sensuous.

Kevin has been sweetly insistent on making love right then, and his kiss brought Molly with him. There was urgency to their lovemaking this time, as if Kevin needed more from her than her physical caresses. His adoring eyes watched her throughout and Molly matched his passion with delight. In the blissfulness that followed, their bodies caked with cornstarch and their hearts still pounding, Kevin asked Molly to enact the Goddess to his Sun God in this year's ritual. No wonder he had come home so playful tonight! He had just learned that he had been chosen as this year's Sun King.

Having attended this ritual for years, she knew what this meant; that what they had just reveled in together would be required for their community magic. Much as she wanted to keep saying yes to her man tonight, she hesitated. She needed time to think it through. This was no small thing. It was a great honor to be asked to channel the Divine Couple in the ritual that celebrated the height of the solar year, but   before she answered, Molly wanted to make sure she could fulfill his request with her whole self. She knew being chosen had been a possibility. They participated each year, were active members of their spiritual community, and were of age. But there were so many others who met the same criteria, and the odds were so steep, Molly had safely tucked this possibility into hiding.

She hardly slept that night, and spent a lot of it watching Kevin slumber. Despite a days' growth of beard, he looked so boyish when he slept, his expression peaceful, his chest rising and falling in rhythm with his breath. Resting her eyes on her lover, a dab of corn flour still stuck to the skin of his forearm, Molly felt as if she had never loved anyone or anything more. What would it mean if she declined? Could she disappoint him? How might that affect their relationship? Or her standing in the community? She had never heard of anyone declining this honor. Did she have the courage to be the first?

She tried to suppress her doubts, but finally she let them rise to the surface. What if she froze at the last minute? What if she was not adept enough at channeling the divine to perform the ritual role without being self-conscious? One had to essentially leave oneself behind, to let oneself become like a hollow bone for the spirit of the divine to flow through. Would her personal shyness dissolve enough when the time came to allow this to happen? These questions and more rolled through her mind one after another and each time she had a different answer, finding no resolution.

Finally she asked herself the most important question, the question that was not about Kevin, or about anyone else. She asked herself whether she could fulfill the role of the Goddess in perfect love and perfect trust. Could she, would she, allow the divine to come through her in service for the highest good of all? She would always regret if she let this spiritual opportunity go. When all the doubts and questions finally silenced, at her core, Molly knew she would tell Kevin yes. Kevin's smile the next morning was worth the sleepless night. Between then and now, Molly's resolve came and went again and again. She felt as if she was walking in a dream, following one step after the next, until her feet brought her here this morning to prepare the meadow with her friends for the sacred rite of Litha.

The drummers walked toward the meadow, mostly young teens, boys who had already taken off their shirts in the growing heat of the day, girls with their hair tied up off their necks. The women moved as one, filling in the northern arc of the circle.

It was traditional that the eldest in the community headed the processional that came next. This special honor belonged to Marian and Robert, their adolescent granddaughter pushing his wheelchair as if it were a throne. The line continued in age order, with all the rest of the elders in the community, mature men and women holding the babes in arms and toddlers too young to make the walk. Younger boys and girls skipped ahead, running to find a spot at the circle's edge. The drum roll continued; a tight rhythm renewed over and over again, underscoring the procession as it snaked into the meadow from the east and made its way deosil in a wide path around the center. Their circle was cast in perfect love and perfect trust.

Once the elders were in place, once the children were seated at their feet, once the drummers had filled in the southern arc of the circle, the lead gave the call, a wild guttural yelp accompanied by a different drum pattern, shorter, staccato, and unmistakable. The drumming suddenly stopped, but the energy hung in the air, the feeling of anticipation certain and sharp. In the silence that followed, the drummers stepped into two straight lines facing one another, creating a corridor between them. The lead began a new rhythm, a simple rumba.

Boom, boom, boom cha! Boom, boom, boom cha!

Now the men in their prime entered the circle through the corridor of drummers. All shapes and sizes, stepping in rhythm to the music, smiling broadly, they entered the circle proud and sassy.

They were bare-chested and all wore the usual costume: dark brown trousers and the rest of their bodies painted green or brown for the Green Man or Horned One. A huge cry erupted from the crowd at the sight of them, cheering them on, pouring out their love and excitement on the sound of their voices.

Molly swayed back and forth to the rhythm, clapping her hands with the rest of the women, knowing that Kevin, as the Sun King, would be the last to enter the circle.

When he stepped into the circle, the only one painted gold, the drumming intensified and another surge of cheering rang out from the crowd.

At the sight of him, several of Molly's friends exclaimed loudly, one came up and hugged her from behind, then removed her cloak to reveal the stunning silver gown that swathed her body and shimmered in the sunlight. Many turned toward her and reverently curtseyed, acknowledging the Goddess for the first time in the ritual.

Kevin looked around until he spotted Molly and his radiant smile widened as he danced toward her and took her hands.

All at once Molly's shyness doubled and thickened as all eyes turned toward them. Stage fright gripped her. The Sun King in all His radiance stood before her, His eyes locked on hers.

He was so handsome. His teeth showed even whiter against His gold painted skin. She felt the familiar surge of desire for Him and He laughed out loud, although no one could hear it above the drums. The Sun King gently but surely began to pull her toward the center of the circle. For a moment, her feet felt truly rooted and she tried to hold her ground, beginning to giggle despite herself.

Kevin, the man inside the King, knew his woman. He knew this moment was a tough one for her, one that would decide whether she was going to see it through or not. A prolonged display of hesitancy would not serve the ritual, so he took swift and decisive action. He reached down around her legs and lifted her up in one smooth action, and everyone whooped and yelled at the sight of it. She flung her arms around his neck and buried her face there, hoping to look like she was kissing his neck instead of hiding her face. He walked to the center and gently set her on her feet. Her face was smeared with gold from his body and Kevin thought she had never looked more beautiful.

Now Brian, last year's Sun King, came forward and handed Kevin the Goddess crown, made of the moon and silver stars. The Sun King crowned the Goddess and then sank to one knee before Her.

Everyone witnessed as the glamour began to work.

Molly stood taller, the tension in her body slackened, and she smiled from her soul. Amanda, last year's Goddess, came forward and handed Molly the crown of the Sun King, a shining gold circlet that shimmered in the light of noon.

Molly had watched this part of the ritual many times and had never imagined herself doing it. And now that she stood there, in the center, holding the crown above Kevin's bowed head, she heard the drumming stop and felt time stand still. She felt the rush of power surge through Her, both down from the Moon and up from the Earth, and heard Her own voice as if from very far away, ringing clear and strong among the hushed crowd.

"I crown you Sun King!"

The drumming started again as everyone cheered and the Sun King rose to the full height of His power.

As if on cue, everyone turned to face the East and Air, and then South and Fire, West and Water, and North and Earth, singing the invocations to each direction and element in unison.

Spirits of the Air, carry me.
Spirits of the Air, carry me home.
Spirits of the Air, carry me home to my heart!

When everyone turned toward the center, Molly and Kevin, the Goddess and God, clasped hands and spun in a circle as everyone sang to them. Molly was aware only of the face of her Consort, sharp and focused in front of the blur of faces as they leaned away from one another spinning, centrifugal force keeping them on their feet. As the invocation ended and the drumming rhythm shifted, they slowed to a stop and a distant part of Molly's mind noticed that everything and everyone beyond the radiant presence of the Sun King before her was still a blur! She did not indulge the part of her that wanted to understand why this was happening, rather, she was grateful to feel this altered state and let it be.

Kevin had not let go of her hands and they stood facing each other as the rest of the crowd shifted into two circles; the men standing around them facing outward and beyond them, another circle of the women facing in. Then the chant and circle dance began.

As the inner circle of men stepped toward the women in rhythm to the drumbeat, they sang:

We are the Seed Sowers, we give love!
We are the Horned One, Sun God above!

Then the outer circle stepped forward to meet the men as the women sang:

We honor the Sun, we honor the fire,
We honor you, brother, we honor desire!

The women continued forward as the men stepped back, the pattern of the dance forming as they sang:

We are the fruit bearers, we give birth.
We are the Mother, the Moon and the Earth!

To which the men responded:

We honor the Moon, we honor the fire,
We honor you, sister, we honor desire!

This chant and dance had been a part of the Litha Sabbat for years, but there were always newcomers to the circle and so it took a few rounds until it caught and the energy began to flow smoothly and comfortably through everyone.

Then came the unmistakable point in the ritual when the energy shifted, as if a key had clicked open the lock and the portal opened. The energy rose and swelled through the sacred space, the flow established itself, and everyone relaxed into it. They stopped concentrating so hard on the words of the chant and the steps of the dance, feeling at one with life and love and blissfully surrendering to the power of the magick.

As the dance went on, the pulse of the dancers stepping in and out, toward and away from the Goddess and God in the center heightened the spell that Molly and Kevin found themselves within. Each time the circle danced forward in honor, hands reached out to caress the honored. Eyes lit, breath quickened as voices sang out. Some kissed each time the dance brought them close enough to do so and the drums slowly increased in volume and tempo.

Kevin took Molly's face in his hands and tilted it up for his kiss. As he watched her eyes, he told her "I honor the moon, I honor your fire, I honor you, my love, and all our desire."

He let his hands run down her neck to her breasts and Molly responded "I honor the Sun, I honor your fire, I honor you, my love, and all our desire!"

Hot sweetness poured through her. Kevin's bold hands had set them both aflame and the energy of the circle lifted them higher. Molly couldn't help furtively glancing out at the circle of dancers and drummers and those at the edge of the circle, momentarily becoming the shy woman she had always been. But everyone seemed lost in their own reverie, given to the moment. Even the elders no longer able to dance seemed to be lost in the music, singing their hearts out with the children. No one was watching her in judgment. In fact, she and Kevin were virtually hidden by the circle of dancers around them.

The feel of Kevin's fingers catching her nipples brought her back to the moment, and she let the last vestiges of reserve slip away. She nodded yes to him and returned his kiss. She could feel the hardened phallus of the Sun God and thrilled to the knowledge that She, as the Goddess, had elicited this from Him. Suddenly, the full meaning and purpose of her role exploded in her every cell, and she allowed the music and the feel of him and her own desire to seize the magick at last. The energy of the circle, the exposure to the elements, standing in the center of their spiritual community, all contributed to the transcendence from a woman and a man making love to the union of Goddess and God.

The kiss of the Sun was hot and the Goddess swooned, Her knees buckling. The God caught and lifted Her up off the ground, their mouths still clinging. She wrapped Her legs around His waist and Her arms around His neck.

We honor the Sun, we honor the fire…

The Goddess clung to the strength of the God, freeing his hands to pull the front of Her skirt up and out of the way. The rest of the fabric draped down behind Her, veiling the intimate contact between them. He freed Himself next and placed Himself, erect and hard up along the belly of the Goddess. She reached one of Her divine hands down to f e e l the velvety softness of His skin, making the eyes of Her God smolder. He lifted Her higher by the hips, She positioned Him perfectly and He lowered the Goddess onto Himself, Her body the Earth, His body the plow making way for the seed.

We honor the Moon, we honor the fire…

The Goddess and God matched the rhythm of the chant. It was the very rhythm of life; of the fertile Earth whose wet soil, warmed by the Sun, becomes the sacred womb for life to blossom. It was the rhythm that matched the heartbeats of every animal of the fields and forests, the flow of the rivers and waterfalls, the lift of the pollen wafting on the breeze, the speed of swallows swooping through the air. It was every rhythm ever felt, the seasons changing, hard work and deep rest, birth and death, and it was nothing less than pure love.

The energy of the circle quickened in the pattern of the dance, in and out and in again. Everyone sang with full voice, alive with the magick between the worlds. The Goddess and God became pure love in the center. He gave to Her, each thrust His all, and She drew from Him, receiving. The dancers stomped the ground, voices ringing, drums booming. The pace grew frenzied now, as the climax took Them together, the cacophony of sound meeting up to one single note, releasing the cone of power in unison. Voices swelled in wordless harmony. And then the silence was deafening as the energy crackled in the air.

Still pulsing together, the God took hold of His Goddess and let Her down to the ground. He held Her eyes with His, Her body close until He was certain She stood firmly on Her feet. Raising Her hands high over Her head, the Goddess cried, "As the Goddess is to the God!" and the God responded "As the God is to the Goddess" and together the two proclaimed "So the two conjoined bring blessedness to life!" They followed this with another deep kiss.

The circle rejoiced, the drumming began again and everyone began to sing:

We are a people in the full height of our power,
This is the place and now is the hour.
We recognize our sacred worth.
We have the power to transform the Earth!

The celebratory chant was sung repeatedly as two children- a maiden and a lad- made their way through the crowd toward the center, he carrying a platter of corn bread and she a bowl of blueberries. They held them before the Goddess and God, who fed one another saying "May you never hunger and may you never thirst!" Once they did so, they turned to the children. Molly's memory flashed. She had been the maiden so many years ago who had brought the blueberries to the Goddess. She remembered being proud, frightened, excited and embarrassed about her part for the ritual. She also remembered the feeling of enchantment when the luminous Goddess had placed the big, sweet berry in Her mouth, and the feeling that shook her when She winked at her.

Perhaps deep inside she had known from that moment, that she would be the Goddess in this ritual one day. But whether she did or not didn't matter as much as wanting to make this moment memorable for the dark-eyed maiden who stood before her now. "May you never hunger!" she said, and placed the berry in her mouth with a wink.

Lughnassad

LUGHNASSAD IS THE SABBAT of the first harvest of the grains. In the heat of Summer it might be difficult to accept that the first of August begins the season of Autumn, but the Wheel of the Year tells us it is so. The Earth is full and lush with Summer's bounty now, and gardeners everywhere are enjoying the first fruits of their labor. Because Pagan spirituality embraces polarity as the balance that holds the world together, rather than as factions that oppose one another in conflict, the celebration and gratitude for the harvest is accompanied by the acute understanding that each time we harvest one of the Earth's growing things we are, indeed, giving it death. Therefore, an additional theme of this sabbat is one of sacrifice, something that is given up for a sacred purpose.

At Litha, the Summer Solstice, Lugh the Sun King reaches His zenith of power and radiance. During the next six weeks until Lughnassad and on through Mabon, the life force of the Sun is poured down onto the growing Earth, His energy feeding the crops.

Slowly, the days begin to shorten in length and we understand this shift as the Sun King's selfless sacrifice. He gives his life for the highest good of all. Pagans celebrate this sabbat by baking and eating bread, often in the shape of the God or the Sun. I believe this was the ancient precursor of the sacrament of Communion.

Under the best of circumstances, a sacrifice is a conscious and deliberate act one chooses to make: giving death to one thing so it can feed the life of the next. The cyclical pattern of Nature models this for us year after year. But sometimes the sacrifice of something precious is not our choice. Sometimes the mysteries of life and death are suddenly and unexpectedly thrust upon us and we deeply mourn what is sacrificed. This story illustrates the complexity of the theme of sacrifice, our understanding of what must be given to keep the sabbats holy, and the healing power of the freshly prepared first harvest.

THEY'D ARGUED LAST NIGHT. It started when Pete called to invite him to go fishing in the morning. Bob was going, too. John gladly accepted, and they agreed to pick him up at 4:00 in the morning so they could get to the river as the sun rose. When he hung up the phone, Cherie asked who had called. When he told her, her face clouded over.

"But tomorrow is Lughnassad!" she exclaimed. "We need to do our harvest rites."

"Can't you do them yourself?" John asked. "It means more to you anyway."

She stared at him for a moment, then turned her back and walked into the kitchen.

"What?" he called after her. "What's wrong?"

She didn't respond right away and John could tell she was holding her tongue.

"Fishing?" She asked, turning toward him. "You want to go fishing with your friends on the holy day instead of sharing the first rite of harvest with me?"

"Don't be like that," he replied. "Fishing is harvesting, just from the water, instead of the soil." The thought of sitting quietly in Pete's boat, sipping from a thermos of coffee in the morning stillness, sounded so good. He hadn't been able to go all summer for one reason or another, and he desperately wanted to go now.

"Can't we do it together on Sunday instead?"

"Can't you go fishing on Sunday?" Her voice rose a bit.

"No. Pete's going tomorrow and it's his boat."

"But, John," Cherie said, sounding hurt. "We always do our ritual together on Lughnassad. We agreed to do this tomorrow when we talked about it last weekend. I can't believe you would just drop our plan like that and agree to go with Pete without talking with me first."

"I forgot," he said, which was a lie. "What's the big deal? It can wait one little day. Or you can do it without me, I won't mind."

"That's not the point," she said. "I don't want to do it alone. Besides," she said, her voice taking on an angry edge, "you don't move the sabbat for your own convenience. They fall where they fall and we shape our lives around them, not the other way around!"

They stood there facing each other for a moment. She kept expecting him to say, "You're right. It's

Lughnassad and we always harvest together. I'd rather do that. I'll call Pete and cancel." But he didn't.

He kept expecting her to say, "You're right. You haven't gone fishing all summer and I can harvest on my own." But she didn't.

Finally, with the discordant silence between them, Cherie turned from him. The only sound filling the space was the clatter of the dinner dishes as she put them in the kitchen sink.

John watched her stand there, tight and upset, and considered this predicament. He was torn between wanting to make it right between them and wanting to have his way. He sighed. Then he walked into the kitchen, the sound of the running water obscuring his footfall so she didn't know he was there. He cleared his throat loudly to get her attention.

"Look," he said, "can't we start a little later in the day? I can be home by one or two and we'll harvest then."

"No!" she spat. Cherie had looked forward to their planned magick all week. She had imagined them starting the day making love, then reviewing the plan for their ritual over breakfast and working together in the garden, side by side in shared spiritual practice.

She turned the faucet off and rested her dripping hands on the edge of the sink.

"I'm not waiting more than half the day for you to finish playing with your friends to begin the sabbat ritual. You either want to do this with me, or you don't!"

"I'm just trying to find a compromise!" John spat back, angry now at Cherie's all-or-nothing-at-all ultimatum.

And then the phone rang. They looked at each other. It rang again.

Cherie shook her hands over the sink, grabbed the dishtowel, and picked up the phone.

"Hello?"

John watched her face as it registered the news.

"I'm on my way," was all she said, and hung up. "Stacy's gone into labor, three moons early. I have to go."

"Wait a minute, he said. "You can't just—"

"I have to go now!" She spoke over him grabbing her keys and her midwife bag from the hall closet, and without looking back, left John standing there, his mouth open.

"Now what?" he thought. "What do I do now?" He could only think of one thing, so he turned the faucet back on and finished the dishes. As he scrubbed and rinsed and stacked, he fumed.

He fumed at Cherie's lack of understanding. He wanted to go fishing. She didn't care. They could start later, but she wouldn't. She wouldn't budge, so he had to miss the one thing he had wanted to do all summer. Soon he would have no more chances to go this year at all. What did he care about the harvest? You harvest when things get ripe, not when the calendar says it's time. They could easily do it Sunday, but Cherie was too stubborn to see reason and make it a win-win.

He fumed when he thought of Pete and Bob enjoying the river, while he'd have to pick the stupid corn and call it religion.

As the evening wore on, he fumed at how Cherie had just dropped everything and ran in the middle of their fight. If he didn't know better, he'd have thought the whole thing was planned.

But even in his anger, he knew that no one plans to deliver their baby prematurely. Even in his anger, he knew what being a midwife means; it means stopping your own life at a moment's notice when duty calls. Even in his anger, John was amazed at how Cherie seemed to do that so easily.

And then he fumed at what he came to at the end of all his fuming. He fumed at the truth—that he had better call Pete and cancel.

The next morning, sweat trickling down his face woke John. He opened his eyes and registered that Cherie still had not returned home. Wow, it must have been a tough night. He wondered how everyone at the birth was doing.

He rose out of bed to put on the coffee. Then he stood under cool water in the shower until he felt fully awake. In the kitchen, he popped some bread in the toaster. Spreading blackberry jam from last year's harvest preserves, he mentally checked off picking the juicy berries today, too. He took a sip of coffee to wash the toast down his throat. There was a lot to do. If he was going to do it, he'd better get started. He reached for his garden hat and stepped outside.

The hot sun shimmered in waves that broke on the rock walls of the garden beds. By the time he reached the corn patch, he was pulling his sweaty tee shirt away from his back. Rotating their crops even in this smaller suburban garden, they had planted the big patch with corn this year. The bed was ten by ten feet and they had planted rows of ten. The majestic stalks never ceased to amaze him. So sturdy and tall. So regal looking.

When they'd put the heirloom seeds in the ground on Mother's Day, he imagined about 200 ears that he'd eat, share, dry and preserve. But many stalks didn't make it. Now he knew not to plant so many cosmos between the rows until the corn was taller. Although the cosmos kept the earwigs out of the cobs, the flowers grew faster than the corn and choked too many of the young plants. Next year he'd know better.

He stepped into the bed to get a closer look. He searched for that one cob, the biggest, fattest, densest corn cob in the patch. This ritual of Cherie's grandmother's had become theirs now. Before you take any off the stalks, you place a small paper sack over the best ear of corn in the garden and tie the bottom around the cob with string. And then let it sit until Mabon. The sack keeps the moisture out and the kernels begin to dry in the summer sun. Six weeks later you take the ear off the stalk. Bang it against something solid and the kernels drop off into the bag and you have next year's seeds for planting.

But it was more than just putting a paper sack on an ear of corn. It was the rite that began the first harvest, the sabbat of Lughnassad. He walked through the rows of corn towering over his head, his feet meeting the morning damp earth, leaving his footprints behind. It smelled green in here, green and hot. He waved away the spider webs as he went and knew he should start singing. Usually Cherie sang; he joined in from time to time, but she carried the chant. Still, she wasn't here today, was she? He should at least try. The good news was that he was alone and only the spirit of the corn, the clever spiders, and the industrious bees would hear him.

Horned One, Lover, Son,
Leaper in the Corn!
Deep in the Mother,
Die and be reborn.

He sang softly, half humming, half singing words and as he went, his eyes assessed each stalk, mentally comparing one ear of corn to another. By the time the chant had taken on a life of its own, by the time he had forgotten he was singing at all, he had narrowed it down to a few ears to choose from. Although the center cob was not the biggest, it was the fattest and he liked that it stood in the middle. He stood there singing to it. It stood there and listened. Man and corn encountered one another in the heat of Lughnassad morning.

It was time to speak the prayer Cherie had written a few years ago that would precede the first act of harvest, the act of giving death to the living corn. He had picked it up from the altar in the living room earlier and now he took it out of his pocket. He spoke the words aloud in a soft voice.

121

"Radiant Sun King, thank you!
We are grateful for your bounty.
Look at our garden, look at this corn!
It is beautiful.
It is healthy.
We have grown it in compost made right here
on this small bit of land we call home.
Its heirloom seeds go back hundreds of years
and not a chemical drop was used to help it along.
We planted, tended, sang and prayed to You,
Sweet Lugh,
As the seeds yielded to stalks,
As the tassels swayed in the breeze,
As the leaves splayed out, and the cobs appeared,
As the corn grew,
We have prayed for this healthy harvest.
Sun King, Radiant One of Light,
Of unconditional light and heart,
You who pour Your life force down upon the Mother,
You who shine down on the flourishing earth,
We give thanks for the bounty that will feed our
family.
Sun King of the great Sacrifice,
We know that as we harvest Your bounty,
We also give You death.
Thank You for Your death
So that we may live.

Blessed Be!"

He was drenched in sweat now. It struck him that Cherie had written the prayer from both of them. He felt his heart soften toward her as he gently pulled the husk from the cob he had selected. It was gorgeous. Golden yellow kernels emerged in almost perfect rows down the middle of the fat cob. It smelled sweet and felt warm in his hand. When the cob was shucked, he placed the paper sack over it and tied it closed with string. He used three knots; one for the Maiden, one for the Mother, and one for the Crone.

Now the true harvesting could begin. He walked to the garden shed, took the big basket they always used, and returned to the west side of the patch. The chant began again in his head and soon found its way out of his mouth. Stalk by stalk, John chose the ripest ears, and soon the crunching sound of corn being torn from its stalk kept the percussive rhythm for the chant.

Horned One — crunch — Lover, Son — crunch —
Leaper in the Corn — crunch — Deep in the
Mother — crunch — Die and be reborn — crunch!

He worked his way widdershins around the patch, dropping the corn into the basket and soon it was close to full. He carried it to the picnic table under the big apple tree. He sighed as the leaves took the direct sunlight off his body.

Sitting in the blessed shade, he wondered how his kids were doing at summer camp. Then he wondered how Cherie was doing and if that baby had been born yet. What a hot day to be in a prolonged labor!

Thirsty now, he went inside to fill a pitcher with water and ice, took a glass, and returned to his garden before the coolness of the house stole his resolve to get back to work. As he sipped, he surveyed the garden. There were blackberries, yes, and also string beans and tomatoes to take in. Lots of herbs were ready to be cut and hung to dry. He knew the berries were next and he dreaded putting on the long sleeves required to protect his arms from the voracious thorns. But experience had made him wise, so he went to do it, then got the ladder and slung it over his shoulder.

John guessed this whole back yard had once been overrun with blackberry vines, which were now carefully tamed and cultivated to grow just by the fence. Several rogue vines still grew within the tall green wall of laurel that created the fence between the back of his yard and his neighbor's. And, of course, the biggest and most beautiful berries grew up where his ladder couldn't reach. "Birds'll get 'em.", he thought.

After the ladder was in place, he went back into the kitchen to get the big metal bowl. They'd stained and ruined enough baskets in the past with berry juice and he congratulated himself for remembering. Within minutes of starting to pick, his fingers were dark purple—that is, where they weren't mixed with his red blood from pricking them with thorns. "Blackberries are smart." he thought. Even the undersides of the leaves, where the best berries hide, are thorny. He picked and cursed at the pain and sang softly as the bowl filled.

Horned One Lover, Son
Leaper in the Corn
Deep in the Mother,
Die and be reborn.

The sun crept higher in the sky. John worked for hours, until finally he bundled and hung the last of the comfrey to dry. He admitted to himself that he felt a great sense of satisfaction. As he sipped another glass of cold water, he looked at all he had accomplished; the corn, the berries, the string beans, some early tomatoes, the herbs. And even more than this collection of garden goodness, was his awakened sense that his day had been spent not only on practical things, but on holy things. That his hard work in the heat of this day had been spiritual.

Sometime during the hours of cutting and picking and gathering, it had ceased to be work. He had entered into the place Cherie always called "between the worlds", a numinous place where you have not actually left your body, but you no longer experience being alive the same way. Where a part of you watches your own berry-stained fingers reach for another tomato, as another part of you hears your own voice chanting. It wasn't feeling separate so much as it was embracing another part of who you are. John no longer felt self-conscious singing the chant out loud, and he no longer felt a trace of the resentment that accompanied him to sleep last night. His thoughts went to Cherie again, and he wondered how things were going for her.

The sun was way past its zenith now; he figured it had to be at least three o'clock. He could feel the weariness of his body and knew he should bring this day of harvest to a close, but there was one more thing to do. He went into the garage, lifted the heavy cast iron cauldron and carefully brought it out, setting it on the slate slab positioned in the center of the yard for just this purpose.

"Why didn't I do this earlier before I was so wiped out?" he asked himself. Grunting as he set the cauldron down, he took two sheets of the newspaper stashed inside it and crumpled them into loose balls. He went back into the garage and took a small bundle of the dried thyme hanging from the rack and put it in the cauldron. Then he walked to the small patch of two-foot tall, ornamental black tipped wheat, still green. Taking his clippers out of his back pocket, he crouched down on his haunches so he was eye to eye with the spiky tops. "Thank you for your sacrifice," he whispered to the grain, to the God of the Sun, and to the entire harvest. He cut nine stalks, then found a vine of nightshade climbing in the laurel. He clipped a length that had bright red berries, and used it to tie the wheat together in a bundle.

John reached for the matches in his pocket as he approached the cauldron once more and set one corner of the newspaper on fire. It quickly took, and when the flames rose and engulfed the thyme, sending fragrant smoke wafting skyward, he began the chant again. He placed the wheat, representing the God, in the cauldron, representing the womb of the Goddess.

Deep in the Mother, Die and be reborn.

He stood there watching, chanting, the rising smoke making his eyes water and tears drip down his face along with his sweat. When the cauldron held nothing more than ashes, his chant ended and he looked up to see Pete and Bob standing just inside the garden gate watching him. Pete held up three good sized salmon. John smiled at his friends, picked up the bowl of blackberries, holding it out in offering as he walked toward them.

"May you never hunger", he said.

John was tearing lettuce for the salad when he heard Cherie's car turn into the driveway. She had been gone over twenty-four hours. Now half past seven, the day had cooled a bit. A welcome relief.

As soon as he saw her face, he knew. Her eyes were swollen from crying. She walked into his outstretched arms, all memory of the harsh words exchanged between them gone.

"The baby didn't make it," she sobbed. "Stacy labored all night—and then there was nothing we could do!"

He held her, knowing there was not much he could do either.

"I need a shower," Cherie said eventually. "And I'm starving!"

When she emerged in fresh clothes, her hair still wet, her eyes still sad, John was bringing the fresh grilled salmon, seasoned with their own basil and tarragon, in from the grill. He had set the table for their dinner; a platter of steaming corn sat by a stick of butter. A green salad boasted their cherry tomatoes, and the smell of blackberry pie baking in the oven began to fill the house.

Cherie stood there feeling the beauty of the scene in her bruised heart, the one that beat love for John, the precious man who had done all this to make her homecoming so welcoming. She smiled at him when she noticed the crystal vase holding the black tipped wheat in the center of their table.

Mabon

MABON, THE AUTUMNAL EQUINOX, marks the time of equal day and equal night as we enter the dark half of the Wheel. Now the nights begin to lengthen, sunlight wanes and temperatures cool. The year is aging, the garden offers up her bounty, and harvesting continues.

Maturation is the theme of the following story, whose structure is based on the ancient Greek myth of the great grain Goddess Demeter and her Maiden daughter Persephone. As the leaves begin to turn and the shadows deepen, we learn how the mysteries of love bring courage, and acceptance brings depth to our understanding of destiny.

PHOEBE WAS ALREADY SITTING UP when she awoke. The dream again. She stared unseeing, lingering for a moment in that other world.

In that place, she was old—ageless—and she walked in confidence, feeling the strength of her beloved always just behind her.

In that place, she'd sat in the shadow, tenderly stroking the hair of a weeping woman, murmuring comfort. "Your souls had an agreement," she had told the woman. "He needed to experience what it's like to save himself, and he could never have done that if you hadn't let him get lost. You fulfilled your promise!"

In that place, one vision fractured as another image formed. This time she'd been holding the hands of an old man whose cloudy eyes were trying to blink away confusion. "You are on the other side," she'd said. "You were not conscious at the moment of your death, so you don't know you've died. Your spirit is here now. This is now your home."

And finally, the last thing she remembered was the sound of her mother Denise's sharp cry, piercing her dream, calling her name.

Although the content of her dream changed each time, several aspects remained constant: she always felt the presence of her unknown beloved, she was always in the role of comforter and teacher, and always awoke with the sound of her mother's anguished cry. She took a shuddering breath as full consciousness brought her back to waking reality and the brightening light of morning.

Phoebe, who had the uncanny knack of knowing what people thought and what they would say before they said it, had told no one about these dreams, not even her mother. People thought she was weird enough already and she made them uncomfortable. Shy and serious as a child, Phoebe remained soft-spoken as she grew, with few friends. She preferred the company of one or two over that of a crowd. Because she always held herself back, her classmates failed to notice her quiet beauty. That was fine with her. The silly social customs of those her age never inspired her. She was grateful for her best friend Helen, who understood her.

Phoebe pulled the covers away and stood up. It was the first day of school.

Helen's parents had recently bought her a car, and now that Phoebe was a senior, she had permission to ride with Helen to school. She felt a bit superior, sitting in a car with the music blasting, passing the school bus on the way.

Phoebe and Helen pulled into the student parking lot. As they left the car, they spotted their friend Gabby getting out of the passenger seat of a black Mustang. They hadn't seen her all summer, and after greeting one another, Gabby said, "Oh, this is my brother Hank," pointing to the driver side window. Hank opened the door and got out, which surprised his sister. He had offered to drive her to school, but the last thing she expected was for him to want to meet her friends.

Phoebe looked at Hank, and when their eyes met, something happened inside her. She felt as if she already knew him, as if somehow he belonged to her. He was tall and powerfully built, and looked more like a man than a boy. Dark locks curled around his ears and his deep-set eyes gave his face a penetrating look, an unusual handsomeness.

"This is my friend Phoebe." Gabby said. Hank took Phoebe's hand and didn't let go. "Hi," Phoebe managed to say.

"And this is my friend Helen," Gabby's voice barely broke through.

Hank replied, "Hi," but he didn't take his eyes from Phoebe's.

"Well," Gabby said after a few seconds of silence while she and Helen stood there, watching Hank and Phoebe gaze at one another. "We'd better get going. Thanks for the ride, Hank."

After a few steps, they realized Phoebe was not walking with them. Turning, they saw Hank kissing Phoebe's hand.

"Come on, Gabby," Helen said. "They've got something going on over there, and I want to get to my locker and class on time for once."

"How is it we've never met?" Hank asked.

"I don't know," Phoebe said. "I didn't even know Gabby had a brother."

"Well, I'm him." "Yes."

"Want to get out of here?" "Sure."

Hank walked around to the passenger side and opened the door for her. She hopped in, and in the few seconds it took for him to come around the car and get in himself, her mind went racing. "What are you doing?" she asked herself. "It's the first day of your senior year! You should go inside. Are you crazy? You don't even know this guy or where he wants to go! Get out of the car! Make a date for another time! What are you doing?" But she didn't move.

Hank got in and released the lever to push his seat as far back as it would go. He turned to Phoebe, and lifted her up onto his lap. Then he kissed her. Phoebe felt as if his kiss was quenching a thirst she didn't even know she'd had. When it ended, their eyes rested on one another's for a moment before he lifted her back into her seat, adjusted his own, started the car, and drove them away.

"I never thought I'd find you," he said.

At the end of the school day, Helen asked Gabby if she had seen Phoebe, and a pinprick of worry pierced her when Gabby said no.

"I wonder where she is." Helen asked. "It's not like her to skip school."

Gabby shrugged. "I bet she took off with Hank. He thinks he's such a lady's man, although as far as I know, he's never had a serious girlfriend. He's been traveling since he graduated from college last May. Anyway, so what? Nothing really happens on the first day anyway. Phoebe didn't miss anything."

Helen drove Gabby home. Her worry grew when they got there and Hank's car was not in the driveway.

After Phoebe left for school, Denise went to her constant sanctuary, the garden, where she felt the most at home, where she poured her passion, where she derived the most pleasure. Nature was everything to her, and she shared and instilled her love of it in her daughter from the start. In mid-spring when Phoebe had been no more than three, Denise sat her down in the garden and let her touch, toss, dig, and even taste the soil, reveling in her daughter's sensuous and direct experience of the Earth. Denise showed Phoebe how to poke her little finger in to make a hole, how to drop a radish seed into it, and watched the clumsy release of several seeds at once.

"That will be a lesson in thinning," she thought, praising her daughter's work.

A few moons later, they had harvested the radishes and eaten them, warm in the sun, right there in the garden. It was Phoebe's first experience of how spicy the vegetable could be. Her eyes had flown wide before tearing up, her nostrils flaring. She broke into a rare smile, and reached for another. All Summer, Denise and Phoebe tracked the growing things in the garden, and in late Autumn, Denise explained why the artichoke plants were withered as she cut the last browning leaves down to the stump. She told her the artichoke needed to go to sleep through the

Winter, but it would awaken at the Vernal equinox and grow tall and abundant once more. The following Spring, Phoebe came running in to the kitchen through the back door, breathless, the light of wonder in her eyes.

"The plant is back!" she said. "In the garden. Without seed, just like you said!"

Denise knew the foundation of the mysteries of life, death and reincarnation had been set. In the years to come, as the Wheel of the Year turned, Denise taught Phoebe all about how to grow food in season. She taught her all about the blood mysteries, all about the cycles of nature, all about the soul's journey from lifetime to lifetime.

Denise was a woman of great influence. Her family went back generations in this town and her estate was wealthy. She owned the very land the town had grown on, and her wealth supported the hospital, library, many of the local farms, and most especially, the schools. A fair and practical woman, Denise's power was a quiet truth rather than an elaborate show. Her beautiful home was neither ostentatious nor overly luxurious. Everyone knew her for the great philanthropist she was, but she was most famous for her magnificent gardens. Food, flowers, herbs, orchards, even a few fields of wheat and barley grew with a magick of which only she knew the secret. She did not flaunt her wealth, but made good use of it and never thought she was superior to anyone else. Good manners and respect, reverence for nature, and the wise stewardship of resources were important lessons she made sure to teach her daughter. Pretension was a waste of time and energy. For this reason, Phoebe attended the same schools as the other children.

Denise thanked the late afternoon sun for the ripe tomatoes she placed in her basket as she waited for Phoebe to return home from school. She planned to cook fresh marinara for their pasta at dinner tonight and was just eyeing the oregano when Helen's car turned the corner. She walked to greet them, expecting to see Phoebe; but Helen was alone.

"Is Phoebe here?" Helen asked.

"No. Don't you know where she is? I thought you'd be driving her home."

Denise had imagined the two of them sitting at dinner, Phoebe telling her all that had transpired during the day. Instead, fear licked up within her heart. "I knew it was a mistake to let her drive instead of take the bus!" she thought. "Why didn't I listen to myself?"

She fixed her great eyes on Helen and, taking care to control the rising hysteria in her voice, she asked, "When did you see her last?"

"This morning when we got to school. Our friend Gabby introduced us to her brother Hank, and when I walked into school, she was still talking with him."

"She didn't come inside with you?" Denise asked tightly. "No. I didn't see her all day. I don't know where she went."

Hank drove them right out of town. When Phoebe saw he was steering them onto the interstate highway, she felt a bit of dread at how far this whole thing was going, but also a great thrill at the defiance of it all. She felt so grown up, sitting there beside him, her book bag forgotten on the back seat, and so childish worrying about where they were going and what she would tell her mother. All her thoughts ceased when Hank spoke again.

"I just bought a little place in the woods I'd like to show you. It needs some work but I think it's going to be fine. Okay with you?"

His eyes caught hers again and his gaze melted away her fear. He had a strong and immediate effect on her.

"Okay." she answered.

Hank's place was a big, two story cabin in the woods. They drove a few miles off the narrow paved road along the wooded trail. The forest was thick. Dappled sunlight filtered through the trees and a carpet of already falling autumn leaves crunched beneath the tires. They pulled up and Hank turned off the ignition.

"Stay here for a minute, okay?" he asked, and she nodded. Hank took the six steps up to the cabin two at a time, reaching into his pocket for the key.

Phoebe watched him, her heart pounding. Her eyes slid over his back, his long legs, broad shoulders, the thick black curls of his hair. She was more than just smitten by his looks. She was shaken to her soul. Her face flushed as a pang of desire shot through her.

He disappeared inside. Phoebe took a deep breath, looking around. About twenty yards into the woods several deer had gathered, including a stag with large antlers. A mother raccoon and her kits climbed out from under the cabin porch. Five crows landed on the roof, and a lovely green garden snake wound its way up the pole at the corner of the porch railing. Squirrels chased one another from the trees beside the cabin onto the roof. The forest was alive with animals and they all seemed to be standing there, bidding her welcome. Phoebe was grateful for the distraction while she waited for Hank. He appeared again, and came to open Phoebe's door. She took the hand he offered, and once she was on her feet, they kissed again, the whole length of their bodies pressing together, Desire intensified. He thought he would drown in her softness. She thought she would swoon from the feel of his strength. When the kiss broke, he took her hand and led her inside his cabin. As he closed the door behind them, the crows cawed a joyous laugh, the stag thrust his antlers through the air, and the forest sighed with love.

After awakening from the blissful sleep that followed their lovemaking, Phoebe watched Hank still asleep. She was madly, wildly, and possessively in love. Her eyes drank in every inch of his face: the strong brow beneath thick black eyebrows, the square jaw and swarthy skin, now beginning to show stubble. She gazed for a while at his perfectly shaped lips, restful now. She wanted to taste them again, but didn't. Instead, she crept out from under his heavy arm. Silently, she pulled on his shirt, and barefoot, tiptoed down the stairs to the main floor. She looked out the big back window. Way out behind this cabin she spied the graveyard.

A flood of what she could only call memory flowed through her. The dream! Was that just this morning? It seemed ages ago. She stood there watching through the window, knowing she had to answer her soul's calling.

Finding her clothes and shoes strewn about on the couch and the floor, she smiled. They had come off in a frenzy of passion before Hank carried her up the stairs. As she dressed, her eyes found his thick fleece jacket hanging on a peg by the back door. Stepping outside, she shrugged it on.

All the same animals and more accompanied her through the trees. As she walked, leaves withered, lost their color and fell, thickening the forest floor beneath her feet. The closer she came to the small clearing of headstones, the more the colors of the Autumn forest faded, until she arrived, surrounded by only shades of gray, some deep, some soft, but all of them shadow.

She counted eleven tombstones, three of which were askew and partially obscured by grey, papery leaves. On the western side of the plot was an old hardwood chair, as if someone liked to sit here among the dead. She took the seat. Two large crows flew down and silently placed a circlet made of willow on her head, its last clinging leaves resting regally on her hair. The crows had crowned their Queen.

Phoebe heard the forest grow silent and felt the air grow cold. She blinked, expecting color to return but it didn't. Something moved. At first, she thought it was the stag, who seemed to be standing sentinel at the edge of the cemetery. But when she looked again, everything everywhere was still and silent, except for the wave of energy she could sense coming toward her.

She welcomed it as it approached. "I'm in the dream!" she thought incredulously, as the energy took form and knelt before her. In its gray hands it held out a gray bowl, filled with bright scarlet pomegranate seeds, the only color in the landscape, startling to behold. Phoebe took some of the jewel-like seeds and ate. As she swallowed the tart juice, energy shifted and moved once more until she was surrounded by the spirits of those buried here, all of them looking at her with light shining from their charcoal eyes.

In the next minutes, hours, days, months, for Phoebe could not tell how time ran in this place, she guided and bore witness and comforted the souls of the dead who needed her. A part of her wondered how she knew the mysteries she spoke of with such depth and clarity, another part felt as if she was finally doing what she was meant to do, and didn't question any of it. Engrossed in the work that flowed easily from her heart and soul, Phoebe was gratified by the sweetness of her own true power.

Denise hung up the phone, somewhat relieved to know that Phoebe had not been admitted into the hospital or emergency room. But where was she?

Helen had left, promising to go back to the school to see if she could find Phoebe, and would call the minute she did. Her daughter had so few friends there really was no one else to question.

Denise sat down at the kitchen table and took a deep breath. "Think, think!" she told herself. "Where could she be?" Panic rose as she thought of her beautiful, quiet, responsible daughter, who would never fail to call with her whereabouts. Phoebe, who would never knowingly cause her mother to worry so. Something terrible had happened, Denise just knew it. She finally surrendered to her panic and dialed 911.

"I want to report a missing person," she said to the calm voice who answered.

"Twenty four hours! Why do we have to wait twenty four hours? She could be dead by then!"

At last the tears flowed as the officer on the other end explained that until one full day had passed, a person could not be considered missing, nor could the police take any action.

"We'll see about that!" Denise snapped. "Put me through to the Chief of Police!" After a few minutes of frustration at the run-around, Denise hung up the phone with a bang.

"Oh, Phoebe!" She slumped back into the kitchen chair. She put her arms on the table top and let her head fall as she sobbed.

146

"Phoebe, Phoebe..." she choked as the storm took hold. When at last it stopped, Denise looked up and out the kitchen window at the darkening sky in a world of gray.

Denise didn't sleep that night. As the hours dragged on, between bouts of sobbing with fear and dread, a plan formed in her mind. First thing in the morning, she would call the bank and freeze her funding of everything in this town. "See how far they go without my money!" she thought with grim satisfaction. Even though it was only one in the morning and not yet twenty-four hours, she decided to go to the police station. She knew the chief of police would not be there at this hour, but she would insist that he be woken up and told to come in right away.

Denise's anger flared and the power of it helped her feel better. She would find out who this brother of Gabby's was. Helen had told her that he had not been home after school either. She would have the police do a background check on— Hank, was it?—and wake up his family to get some answers. Why should she be the only one awake and consumed with worry?

Officer Charon was reading a report at the front desk when a woman pounded on the big glass door. She buzzed the door open and remained standing as the woman, whose eyes were swollen from crying, slammed through it. She knew she had seen this woman before but couldn't place her.

"What can I do for you?" she asked.

"Find my daughter!" Denise said, deadly serious. "I want action taken on this immediately!"

For a moment, Officer Charon could swear the woman before her stood about eight feet tall, her voice filling the anteroom. But when she saw the stricken look in her eyes, compassion swelled for the mother whose daughter was lost. Then she realized who Denise was, and became nervous. "Oh, no," she thought. "Why did this have to happen during my shift?" Then she learned that Phoebe was a teenager in high school, and mistakenly said, "Teenagers do all kinds of crazy things! She's probably staying at a friend's house and forgot to call you. Is everything okay at home?"

Denise glared at her and instead of dignifying her question with an answer, said, "I want the Chief of Police contacted right now!"

Officer Charon complied.

Paul Sawicky, the Chief of Police, rapped on the door to Gabby's house. A light went on in an upstairs window a minute before Gabby opened the door. He and Denise entered the foyer asking for her parents.

"My mother is dead and my Dad..." Gabby trailed off. "Dad has Alzheimer's. My sister is here."

After much questioning, they learned that neither Gabby nor her older sister knew where Hank's place was. Their lives were filled with caring for their father. There was no love lost between Gabby and her brother. Her resentment toward him was clear when she told them how he had gone off to college and abandoned them and their father. Gabby was desperately trying to finish high school and even now that he was back, he had bought some place else to live, instead of coming home to help relieve his sisters of some of the burden. They had been so angry when he told them about his plan to live in the new place that they refused to go and see it, or even ask him where it was. All they remembered about it was that it was a cabin in the woods.

Gabby could reveal nothing more than Helen had; she had last seen Hank when, in an uncharacteristic gesture of generosity, he'd offered to drive her to school yesterday morning. Helen had driven her home after school, and that's the last she'd thought about it until now, when they rapped on her door in the middle of the night. She was used to Hank's absence.

Walking out to the car, Chief Sawicky told Denise they'd have to wait until the county records office opened at eight in the morning to look up the purchase of his cabin and get the address. Like a child, Denise stomped her foot in frustrated anger. On the way back to the station, he said he would meet her at the records office at seven thirty instead. He would get someone to open the office early.

It seemed forever until dawn arrived. Denise stood looking out her kitchen window, her arms crossed atop her aching chest as the dim light began to reveal her sleeping garden. At first she thought it was the quality of light that seemed to have washed the color out of the scene before her eyes. Then she thought it must be this upset that caused her to see only the color gray in the world outside her kitchen. But then she realized that everything was colorless. She looked down at her own gray hands, at the newly gray linens on the table, even yesterday's basket of tomatoes. Gray. Everywhere gray.

"That's it," she thought, and said aloud, "I've gone mad!"

By the time Denise arrived at the records office, two clerks were looking for the copy of the deed with Hank's signature and the address. The Chief opened the door for her as she entered the brightly lit, yet fully gray, office.

"Got it!" one of the clerks cried.

As they raced out of town, the sound of the sirens and the sight of other cars pulling over for them soothed Denise a bit. It felt good to finally be in action. She wanted to ask Sawicky if he saw only gray as well, but it wouldn't do to have him know she was losing her mind.

Phoebe looked up into Hank's eyes and felt absolutely adored. They had just come downstairs in what was becoming their pattern: making love, taking a nap, and then having a meal. The kitchen was warm and smelled of roasting chicken and vegetables. Phoebe turned to look outside the window, leaning back onto Hank's strong frame as he put his arms around her and kissed the top of her head.

He could sense that she was already being pulled to visit the graveyard again, and knew he could do nothing to stop her. He wanted to hold her forever within his arms, to possess her and keep her always within his reach. He also knew that he couldn't. As if to affirm this, she slipped from his hold, pulled on his coat and without looking back, exited the cabin. He watched her walk through the gray woods until she disappeared in the trees. He sighed. He'd have to wait. Again.

Phoebe stepped between the worlds to continue her work. She was alive and replete with purpose. She felt the tug of Hank's love and the call of the distant life she had left behind with her mother, but the draw to the souls of the dead eclipsed them both.

The three police cars drove slowly down the wooded trail toward Hank's cabin. The GPS in the chief's car told them they should have arrived. But there was no cabin to be found. Denise wondered if, like her, Sawicky saw only stark, gray, leafless trees as far as the eye could see. The car rolled to a stop and he got out. The others followed. All of them stood there staring.

"What the—" Sawicky swore softly.

"We must have made a wrong turn." Denise said.

They got back in their cars and carefully backed out to the main road. Chief Sawicky punched the address into the GPS again and the exact same directions came back up on the screen. He punched a few more buttons and a map came up instead.

"Okay, let's try again" he said.

They listened to the flat electronic voice instruct them to drive forward and veer left, the directions matching the exact path they had already driven. Denise thought she'd explode when the voice announced, "You have arrived at your destination." This could not be their destination--there was nothing here. They tried again with the same result and Sawicky knew he'd better get Denise out of these woods, because the woman was rapidly becoming hysterical.

Back at the police station, someone put a cup of hot tea in Denise's hand as she sat in the Chief's office, tears streaming down her face. Chief Sawicky sat in front of his computer, doing a background search on Hank. He found nothing unusual. Hank's birth certificate, some hospital records, a school loan.

No record of any arrests, no misdemeanors, no FBI file. There were none in his family either. Just his mothers' death certificate and the deed to the house in town. He was stumped and didn't know what he was going to tell Denise next except to go home and try to get some rest. He promised her he would spare no effort in finding Phoebe and would keep her posted on the progress. There was nothing she could do sitting here. He spoke softly, advising her that it would be wiser for her to be at home in case Phoebe showed up there. He expected Denise to protest, and it was somehow disturbing when she quietly nodded and walked passively with him to his car. He drove her home himself, and had another officer follow them in Denise's car.

When Phoebe returned to the cabin hours later, Hank fed her. They sat at the round table for two and he put small forkfuls of chicken and carrots into Phoebe's mouth until the light returned to her eyes and the color to her face. She swallowed and shook her head at the next bite.

"I have to go to my mother," she said softly.

"Stay the night" he said, his eyes pleading.

She nodded and let him carry her up the stairs.

The next morning they dressed quietly. The drive home before sunrise was difficult. Hank held her hand under his on the stick shift and in this way, Phoebe felt they were both in control of the car as it made its way back out through the woods and onto the main road that led to the highway. She watched all the animals follow them as they retreated, and heard the crows caw loudly as if to alert the soul of the forest that its Queen was departing.

Just before they reached the highway, Hank said, "This can't be the end."

Phoebe assured him, "It isn't."

His jaw relaxed a bit upon hearing her words, but his expression remained unhappy.

When they turned onto the highway, it felt surreal to Phoebe that the world was still going on exactly as she had left it. The car picked up speed. Miles disappeared beneath the wheels. Proximity delivered her mother's pain to her, and Phoebe felt herself colliding with her former life. Only now, she was different. She brought with her a deep and sure love for the man beside her. She brought all her experiences in the cemetery, not just the dreams that had seemed real, but the actual experience of her work with the souls of the dead. She brought with her all she had gained by following her heart, by leaving what had been familiar, by surrendering her body to the heat of love's touch. She had no idea how her life was going to be now that everything had changed. She only knew it was time to return.

At the top of her street, Hank pulled over and stopped the car. They indulged in their last hungry kiss before parting.

Denise was standing at the big front window, staring into the pre-dawn darkness, when she saw the headlights of a car illuminating the street in front of her house. She watched the car that had been described to her as Hank's Mustang, crawl up the driveway, uncertain whether it was real or something she was hallucinating in her exhaustion.

She had imagined over and over what she'd do, what she'd say, how she'd run to pull Phoebe into her embrace when she saw her again, but now she found her feet were rooted to the spot. A steady flow of emotions coursed through her: relief, happiness, rage, a mother's love.

She watched through the window as her daughter's lover got out of his car, ran around to open the passenger side door, and tenderly offered his hand to Phoebe, who emerged into his embrace. Denise heard her own sob when her eyes rested on her daughter's form at last. She stood there regarding them, clinging together in the darkness.

Phoebe released herself from Hank, and said something to him.

He nodded, kissed her, got in his car and rolled back down the drive way into the street.

Phoebe walked to the front door.

Denise noticed that Hank waited for her to open it before he drove away.

Phoebe walked up the stairs to the living room and turned to face her mother.

When their eyes met, Denise's relief caused her knees to give way and she collapsed into the nearest chair. She dropped her face into her hands and let the sobs come.

Phoebe ran to her and knelt at her feet. She put her head in her mother's lap and her arms around her waist.

"Phoebe. Oh, Phoebe!"

"Mom," Phoebe murmured over and over until the sobbing ceased.

At last, Denise looked down at her beautiful daughter, tucking a few strands of Phoebe's hair behind her ear.

"Did he hurt you?" she asked.

"No." Phoebe replied. "He loved me."

"Phoebe," Denise said, the tears streaming again. "Why...? Where...?"

Phoebe answered with the only words she could find.

"It just...happened. I couldn't help it. I didn't want to help it." She swallowed. "The souls of the dead. They needed me. I don't know how, but I knew what to do, so I did. It's different now. I did my own magick, Mom. And Hank? He was why." Mother and daughter sat in the stillness, holding one another. Denise thought her heart would break. She knew she would never hold her daughter as a little girl again. Phoebe had become a woman, and not just because of the boy. Now she carried the light of experienced wisdom in her eyes. Phoebe's gaze met her mother's woman to woman.

157

"I'm home now," Phoebe said. "And the whole way home, all I could think of was your crunchy French toast and applesauce. Will you make some for me?"

Denise's smile broke the grief on her face. "Yes."

It felt good to know Phoebe still needed her for something. They walked to the kitchen together. Light was growing as the sun rose. Denise noticed that color had returned to the world.

Samhain

SAMHAIN IS THE POINT on the Wheel of the Year that ushers in the season of Winter and the darkest eighth of the year. It is said that this is the night when the veil between the worlds is the thinnest, and mortals can more easily reach between the thin layers of reality to connect with their Beloved Dead. Because of this, our Ancestors also extend toward us. The connection through the veil offers us the experience of a great mystery.

The Samhain story that follows brings the reader into this mystery by introducing the concept of reincarnation and transmigration of the soul. It describes an ancient divinatory technique called scrying: the act of gazing into fire or still water or a dark mirror until sight with the eyes gives way to visions within the mind. Mystics and seekers, like the fortune teller gazing into a crystal ball, engage in this practice to receive messages and insight from the spiritual realms. This story brings us to the true meaning of the Hallowed Eve by engaging us in both the sadness of death in this world, and in the continuation of life in the realm of spirit.

I DON'T KNOW WHY I am putting on mascara just to cry it off anyway. But somehow making up my face makes me feel stronger. Or maybe it's the routine of it, this daily task that makes me feel more beautiful, that assures me I can do what is coming next. I grab my coat and wrap my scarf around my neck against the cold and walk to my cat's grave beneath the apple tree in my back yard. This Samhain is my first without her in nearly two decades. I have come to pay my respects, to let everything else fall away and fully think about her, to wholly feel my heart so heavy with love and sorrow. I miss Wanda with her luxurious, black fur, big ruff, and dainty ways, whose still body rests within the earth instead of on my lap. What I wouldn't give to hold her head in my hand and kiss between her ears once more.

On one side of the stone marking her grave grows a long stalk of mullein. On the other is one of comfrey. Strung between them is a huge spider web, the largest I have ever seen. Because it is almost as tall as I am, I can't help noticing the magnificent and intricate detail, how each attachment to the concentric circles is evenly spaced. I am compelled to touch it, and am surprised and relieved to find that it is not sticky, so I don't ruin all of Grandmother Spider's hard work. It is gossamer soft and silky white. It even smells sweet. I wonder at this veil like web. Is it *The Veil* between the worlds?

Pondering this, I spy ghostly shadows beyond her web; three of them around a camp fire on a beach, appearing and disappearing like frames of an old silent movie flickering on the screen, until the images stabilize and I can see them clearly. It's Grandma Fay for sure—I'd know those eyes anywhere— but I don't know the other two. They must be further back in the lost history of my family. The man has the curly hair of my Romanian ancestors and the woman holds a cooking pot in her hand and a long wooden spoon. Her sagging cotton hat falls to one side on her head. She looks extremely dour.

The Romanian bends down to tie his shoe, and I notice it is old and worn. He looks up and smiles at me and I feel...known. He says he has been watching me from the other side for a long time.

He is proud of my work but a bit scared for me, too. My boldness frightens him. He takes out his fiddle, which fits perfectly under his chin. The music is slow and minor, and Grandma, a young woman now with reddish hair, begins to sing counterpart. Her voice is lovely and familiar and it breaks my heart to heart it again.

Come with me to the edge of the sea.
Throw the stone with your wish.
Then we'll dance by the sound of the fire
As it crackles and cooks the fish.
Oh, this is where we meet in love,
And this is where we feast.
Here is where we all will gather,
When the day's complete.

I know this song, yet I have never heard it. My tears fall as the fiddle plays the refrain. Grandma hums softly as she stokes the fire. The dour hat-bearer places her pot on the coals. Then she reaches through the web—I had forgotten it was there—and pulls me through!

All sound stops. I am in a silent movie. I can't hear the music, though they are still playing and singing. I can smell the smoke from the fire. I can feel the heat from the flame.   I can even feel the soft, giving sand under my feet. But I can't hear a thing in the deep silence of the other world.

I turn and look at The Hat. She is looking directly at me, but now appears more serious than dour. I ask, "What happened?" But I can't make a sound, just as I can't hear any. Her eyes soften as if she sympathizes with my dilemma. She knows I won't hear her response.

My knees weaken and I crumple to the sand. The Hat places a warm cup of some steaming liquid into my hands. She is waiting for me to drink, and fearing to refuse, I sip. Clearly my taste buds are still working, because I can taste and smell the salty fish broth. It's good. I sip again and again and I can feel my heart begin to beat more normally.

Grandma and the Romanian have finished their song. I know this because they are now smiling at each other. He lays the fiddle down on a blanket and puts his arm around her. They lean their heads together in love. They have forgotten I am here. This is the grandmother I have missed so much. I want to run and embrace her. But I seem unable to move from my spot by the fire with the cup of broth warming my hands.

The Hat waves at me to get my attention. I see her mouth moving but I can't hear what she is saying. What's the use of coming here if I can't communicate? But she is not frustrated by my lack of hearing or my futile attempts to speak and ask questions. She takes the cup from my hands and walks close behind me and stops. I feel the bones of her knees as they rest on my back.

I sit by the fire and watch the flames. It's warm and cozy in this thick silence and I lean back against The Hat. For the first time since she pulled me through, I completely relax. The fire is beautiful, soft orange and yellow, blue below the glowing embers. I feel as if I could stare at it forever, and so I do. The thought occurs to me that I should look toward my grandmother and the Romanian, should try to talk with them or try harder to listen to what they might want to tell me. But just as quickly, that thought floats away and I become resting flame.

There inside the fire, a scene appears. It's a Winter scene, and I wonder briefly how the ice and snow can remain in the fire. The sun has almost set, the first star shines low in the sky. I hear boots crunching in the snow, and I look down and see that they are mine. I've never seen these boots before but there they are, on the ends of my long legs, walking up the steps to my front porch. I am no longer watching through the flame but standing on the porch in the cold air, my arms full of logs for my fire. Carefully, I drop all but three outside the front door. I watch my own hand as it reaches for the door handle and notice that it is the hand of a man. I lift it to scratch the side of my mouth, and my fingers make contact with my mustache. I'm a man! A cold man who is ready to come into the warmth.

Inside, I smell baking. And there she is. Anna. My bride. The love of my life. When she sees me, she smiles the smile I love so much. Walking to the fireplace, I put the logs down.

Anna comes over to me, kisses my cold cheek, and begins to unbutton my coat. I take it off and hand it to her. How I love this woman. I watch as she walks back to the kitchen and then I turn to place a log on the fire, adjusting it with the poker till flames lick up the sides. I hold my hands out toward the fire and hear her call, "James! Come!" I love to hear her call my name.

In the kitchen, the table is set with the special dishes so I know this is the night of the forecast supper. The number of bay leaves left on the plate will determine the fortune of the coming year. Times have been lean so the stew has no meat, but the potatoes and beets, parsnips and carrots smell good and hearty. My mouth waters at the sight of the steam rising off the fresh baked loaf with the chunk of butter beside it.

We walk clockwise around the table three times. I never remember the details of how this all goes, but Anna always does. When we stop, she lifts the piece of lace from the center of the table and we both hold an edge.

"See how fragile, how delicate, how beautiful," she says. "Such is the fabric of life!"

We lower the lace again and sit. Nothing happens. When I look at her, she smiles at me and I smile back.

Her eyes glance over to the stew on the stove and suddenly I remember. I am supposed to serve her now. The provider goes first! I get up and promptly trip on our thin rug. Embarrassed, I grab her plate and walk to the stove. Taking the ladle, I stir the stew three times and then, without looking into the pot, spoon three ladles full onto her plate. When I place it before her, she gets up to do the same for me. Soon we are sitting at the table with our plates full. My hungry stomach growls and I reach for my fork. Anna gives a small warning cough and pushes the loaf half an inch toward me. Oh, yes. Right. Why can't I remember these things? I cut a slice of bread and hand it to her, saying, "May you never hunger." Then she returns the gesture.

Now we can eat. The talk is the usual, news and gossip. Sarah still won't let Charlie back home, the press is broken so no paper again this week, and old man Barley saw a bull moose with a huge rack behind his barn. We should have meat soon.

I can see three bay leaves already on my plate.

Anna says, "Good thing I pulled the last of the potatoes yesterday before the snow."

A third bay leaf appears on hers. It was under a carrot slice. She smiles. Three for each of us and six altogether. I can see she wants to say something but is holding her tongue. We must wait until we finish the meal before we speculate. I sop up the rest of the gravy with my bread. Anna takes our plates to the sink.

She carefully picks up the six bay leaves and places them on another small plate.

"Let's have our tea by the fire", she says, and the sound of her voice is intoxicating.

I can't help myself. I pull her to me and kiss her. The kind of delicious kiss you feel in your whole body and when it ends, her eyes are shining at me. Anna lifts the plate of bay leaves, takes my hand, and walks us to the fire. She places the plate on the fireplace mantle. We stand in the warmth emanating from the glow.

"Three is such good fortune," she says. "I put the customary thirteen leaves for a year of moons in the stew. Each of us getting three is also good. We are in this together. Six will bring us balance.

169

And James," she says as she takes my hand and presses it low on her belly, "We are soon to be three!"

I blink. Anna's image fades to darkness, and my eyes behold nothing but the fire on the sand. The Hat senses I am back and comes around to face me. She puts the cup of fish broth in my hands again and automatically I sip. A deep breath brings me fully back to her presence. She is looking at me. I feel more comfortable looking back now and so I do. I notice that her eyes are deep brown, and I can see a few dark curls escaping the hat of The Hat. I feel giddy after this vision.

"What's your name?" I try to say to her. "Hattie?" Hysterical laughter shakes my body but I make no sound. Or is it that I just can't hear the sound I make? She watches me as my body stills and the absurd smile melts from my face.

Now my mind starts racing. Who were those two, Anna and James, in the vision of the fire? Why did they—we—appear in such specific detail? Wait! I was in the vision. Wasn't I James? I must have been because I am sure I will never forget that kiss. But then, how could I see the whole thing if I was in the whole thing? Why was the scene I saw—lived—important enough to recall? Why did the vision vanish with the news of the babe within my love's womb? I find myself trying to make sense of all this.

The Hat touches my shoulder and my wandering thoughts gather and focus. Her touch feels both solid and mystical. I feel myself surrender to exactly where I am. No more trying to understand, no more trying to make sense. Just sitting by the fire with my Ancestors, content to be in their presence. The Hat takes my half empty cup, returns behind me, and I lean back as I look into the fire once more.

Just as before, I gaze at the fire and then suddenly, I am living in the scene that just a second ago I glimpsed within the flame. There I am! I am sure the adolescent girl is me, although I don't recognize the place. My long brown skirt and pale yellow apron billow in the wind as I walk down a gentle slope toward the barn. No, it's not a barn. It looks like one but once I walk inside I see the baking ovens and racks, the sacks of flour, salt and seeds. I feel warmth radiating from the ovens. Reaching into my apron pocket, I grab and place my cotton hat on my head, low across my forehead to catch the sweat I know will form shortly. The top of it falls to one side, like it always does.

I spy my black and white cat, not far from the oven, snoozing. He knows he is not supposed to be in here.

"Bowtie!" I shout. "Shoo!"

He languidly raises his head and looks at me as if to say, "Oh, dear, must we do this again?" I lift the broom from its corner and he knows he is about to get swept. I watch him run out, then walk to the oven and open the door. Two more beautiful loaves have browned perfectly. Slipping the bread board underneath, I remove them to cool beside the other loaves on the old wooden table in the center of the room.

A voice calls out from the house. "Butter!"

When I look back through the open door of the bakery, there she is, my Grandmother Anna. She is holding a wooden slab with a brick of butter on it, and her smile lights the day. I lift the long curls off the back of my neck to cool myself as I return her smile.

"Sometimes you look just like your Grandfather", she tells me.

She walks into the bakery and chooses one of the loaves of braided bread, shiny from the brushed-on egg whites and peppered with poppy seeds. Taking the old bread knife off the table, I slice the heel off the loaf. Grandmother's butter melts easily into it as she hands it to me saying, "May you never hunger…"

The vision fades. I am sitting by the fire and the cup is being placed in my hand. I sip. What's in this stuff anyway?

I swallow and look up at The Hat. It's my Hat. Or one just like the one I put on in the bakery. Our eyes lock as the truth explodes in me, filling my heart, touching my soul, overflowing from my eyes. I put the cup of fish broth down. I stand. Unafraid, I turn to face The Hat straight on. We are the same height. For the first time she smiles and all the serious, sour, and somber flees her face. We embrace.

I am in the other world. Of course I am. I suppose I had to know that from the moment The Hat pulled me into it. But I had been so caught up in the soundlessness, the visions in the fire and the taste of the broth in the cup given and taken from my hands that I hadn't really thought about where I was. I shiver as I ask myself if I have just embraced a ghost. I have the risky thought that because I have eaten in this place, like the Greek Maiden Goddess Persephone, I may never be able to leave! There is no Demeter, no Mother Goddess, to call a strike till a negotiation is made to get me back. A cold fright fills my chest as I realize that no one knows I am here.

Wildly, I look over at Grandma and the Romanian. They are sitting close to one another on a log. Not talking now, they sit watching the fire and I wonder what they are seeing in the flame. I stand there looking at them, her arms around her knees, his hands dangling between his. I notice that his nails are too long. Their eyes look empty, still as glass as they stare blindly at the fire.

Oh my Goddess! They are dead! What am I doing here among the dead? Intensely, I wish I wasn't. I have no idea how to leave. My heartbeat quickens as thoughts of being trapped with my dead ancestors fly through my mind. Wait. Wait! I'm still alive! I can still speak and think and feel. I don't belong here. I am not supposed to be here now, or yet. Oh good Goddess, what am I going to do?

And then, very clearly I hear The Hat. I don't see her mouth move as she speaks and yet I can hear her voice. Why can I suddenly hear? Another mystery I put aside to resolve later.

"Dear One", she says, her eyes holding mine. "Please don't be afraid. We share a soul across time. Once you were me and once I will be you and now we share the fire between the worlds. You will not, cannot stay here with me. Don't worry. Your life of television and taking out the garbage and burying cats still waits for you. You'll be back there again, forgetting to buy something at the grocery store, before you know it. For now, watch the fire for your origins. Let the knowing unfold within you and restore yourself with the broth. You are the child of the bay leaf dinner, you are the one who pulled you through to remember, you are the one who longs to go back to your illusion of safety through the veil to the land of hardship—I mean, the land of the living!"

It is such a relief to hear something that I start to cry. This causes Grandma and the Romanian to blink and lift their heads to look from the fire to me. I put my face in my hands and sob, like a little child, my ribs shaking, my breath staccato. I can't stop. It seems like everything I have ever grieved, been sad or upset about is part of this cry, every wrong or injustice I have ever suffered, every time I have been misunderstood, falsely accused, or misrepresented, every deep fear. It's a stormy cry and I am helpless to it. My tears flow like small creeks that pool and swell and pour over to put out the fire. I smell damp smoke and notice that the fire's heat is gone. I lift my head from my hands, open my eyes to find myself sitting, back from between the worlds, before Wanda's grave.

The spider sits motionless in the web she's woven between mullein stalk and comfrey leaf.

Chants Used In The Text

Yule
"Lucina" by Kay Gardener. Words altered to suit the story.

Imbolc
"Oh, Great Mother" by ALisa Starkweather

Beltane
"We All Come from the Goddess" by Z. Budapest

Litha
"We Are the Seed Sowers" by LunaSea Coven
"We Are a People" by Shawna Carol

Lughnassad
"Horned One, Lover, Son" learned at the Boulder, Colorado Pagan Alliance, late 1980's

Acknowledgements

I stand on the shoulders of many strong and courageous women who have reclaimed their place in spiritual leadership. Their modeling and authorship have informed, inspired, and motivated me to create my magickal life and my ministry, and to put my own words on paper. They are: Charlene Spretnak, Z. Budapest, Starhawk, Monica Sjoo, Merlin Stone, and Shekhinah Mountainwater.

Art is not created in a vacuum and no one produces their work alone. For the help, support, and encouragement of the following, I am deeply grateful.

Many thanks to LunaSea and MoonWise Covens for my magickal experiences and spiritual growth with them. To all of my Mystery School students and Initiates who have taught me more than I could ever have taught them. To the Gaia's Temple congregation for showing me how important it is to keep the mysteries intact and alive; thank you for your trust, loyalty and support. I am equally grateful for my family's belief in, support, and loving acceptance of me, exactly as I am.

To Sonya Lea and Pamela Grace in my first writing group, who assured me I was onto something in the early days, and to Elizabeth Zinda and Dawn Dickson in my next writing group for your support as this book was produced and published, thank you. Heartfelt gratitude to the following people who have read, listened, and offered intelligent suggestions as this book was in development: Corbin Lewars, Pamela Gerke, Shelagh Garren, Kris Adair, Manda Levine, Waverly Fitzgerald, and Shawna Carol. Thank you to Patrick Corrigan for your lovely drawings.

I am most grateful to Kitty Honeycutt of Ravenswood Publishing for taking me on and giving me a second chance to bring my stories to the world. Thank you to Loretta Matson for the gorgeous book cover, and to my editor Cindy Wyckoff, who was patient, wise, and respectful, asking all the right questions.

I'd be hard pressed to find a better writing mentor or friend than Sonya Lea. I am forever grateful for your expertise, both expressed and modeled. Thank you for lifting me again and again, and for all the soulful experiences we have shared in friendship.

And when all is said and done, my heart is most grateful to you, Noemi Chaparro, for the love that makes my world go 'round.

Made in the USA
Columbia, SC
14 January 2018